PENGUIN BOOKS

C2038

THE PATON STREET CASE

JOHN BINGHAM

John Bingham, also known as Lord Clanmorris, was born in 1908 and was educated at Cheltenham College and in France and Germany. On the outbreak of war he was called up as a Territorial in the Royal Engineers, and describes his war years as 'undistinguished by gallantry or, indeed, any particular dangers'. He has travelled in many countries and after the war he worked for two years with the Control Commission, stationed at Hanover in Germany.

Much of his life has been spent as a newspaper man, and his work has been published in nine countries. His other books are: *Murder Plan Six* (available in Penguins), *My Name is Michael Sibley*, *The Third Skin*, *Marion*, *Night's Black Agent*, and *A Case of Libel*.

His wife, playwright and authoress, writes under the name of Madelaine Bingham, and they have a son and a daughter.

THE PATON STREET CASE

JOHN BINGHAM

PENGUIN BOOKS

Penguin Books Ltd, Harmondsworth, Middlesex, England
Penguin Books Inc., 3300 Clipper Mill Road, Baltimore 11. Md. U.S.A.
Penguin Books Pty Ltd, Ringwood, Victoria, Australia

—

First published by Gollancz in 1955
Published in Penguin Books 1964

—

Copyright © John Bingham, 1955

—

Made and printed in Great Britain
by Hunt, Barnard & Co. Ltd,
Aylesbury
Set in Monotype Imprint

Chapter 1

IF a disembodied spirit of sardonic temperament, finding time hanging heavily on its hands, had made a rapid tour of London on the hot night of a certain June 5th, he would doubtless have found much to cause him to pause from time to time and give thanks to the Great Eternal for His never-failing compassion and mercy. He would have been grateful, for one thing, that the generality of men and women were unable to see into the future.

In due course, the spirit might have cocked an eye down at Chief Detective Inspector David Morgan, peacefully asleep with his wife, Gwen, in his small house in a Chelsea side street.

He might have felt a strong desire to nudge that sturdy man, and ask him what he meant by sleeping, when events were about to take place which would be of interest to any police officer. There would certainly have been an urge to cry out, though soundlessly and ineffectually:

'You have spent the evening peacefully with your wife, strolling along the Embankment by the Thames in the summer air, but now bestir yourself!

'Fling aside the bedclothes, and dress, and drive quickly to Number 127, Paton Street, Notting Hill Gate, and do not be deterred by the thought that the neighbourhood is unromantic and commonplace. Go, driving quickly through the night in your small private car. The candles are burning low, Inspector, and after the candles will come the flames.'

Passing quickly from above the house of Inspector Morgan, the spirit might have moved only two streets away to a small flat owned by the local authorities.

The rent is low, suitable to the pocket of a Scotland Yard sergeant, but the furnishings and fittings are modern. A modest dwelling, but there is no reason why it should be untidy, and no reason why the breakfast things should still lie unwashed in the sink, unless the housewife is a slut. Can it be that Sergeant Fred Shaw knows it, and won't admit it, because he loves her? Is this why he is speaking hard, bitter words to her, or is it because he is jealous and afraid of losing her?

She's pretty, is Evelyn Shaw, even now, when she is tossing her dark curls, and flashing her brown eyes, and reproaching him for being out on jobs in the evenings, as well as by day, and asking why a girl should not go out a bit herself.

Carry on, Sergeant, quick-tempered, warm-hearted Sergeant Shaw. Have it out with her, if you must. It's not the first time, and it won't be the last. Or will it? It's not worth-while going to bed now, Sergeant. No chance of making it up that way. It is after midnight, and the time is growing short for you, too.

It is quite a way from Chelsea to Ilford, but worth it when you get there, because there is Gladys Turner, in her single bed, and her husband, Len Turner, also in a single bed, and between them is the night table with the reading-lamp.

Len is asleep, because he has just finished a turn as a charge engineer at the power-station. So he's tired out, and he is sleeping peacefully, because he can think of no reason why he shouldn't, poor innocent fellow.

He's never heard of Paton Street, and Notting Hill Gate to him is just a place he passes through when he goes to the dog-racing at the White City.

But Gladys Turner, she knows Paton Street very well indeed. She knows Number 127, too. She ought to, she's been there often enough.

She's not asleep, and nowhere near asleep. She's just lying there, white-faced, staring at the ceiling. Staring and staring, and sometimes trembling a little. Len might have noticed something was wrong, only he was so tired that he went to bed almost as soon as he came home.

Lucky Len. Get some sleep while you can.

So Gladys is alone with her thoughts, and her sleeping husband, and the dark shadows cast by the reading-lamp. It's going to burn all night, that lamp, because it would be worse for Gladys in the dark.

There's not going to be much change here, for a while. It gets boring watching a terrified woman staring at a ceiling, and the journey from Ilford to Hampstead does not take long for a celestial traveller with an inquiring mind.

6

Ho, ho! Now here's a rewarding sight, now here's something really good! Otto Steiner, none other, and Rose Steiner, his wife, and they know all about Number 127, Paton Street, because they have it on a fifteen years lease, and they've been letting off the first floor and using the ground floor for their furniture and upholstery business.

The situation of Otto and Rose Steiner must have made any sardonic spirit hover airborne above them for quite a time and then pass on with a quiet chuckle of pleasurable anticipation.

He would have seen Rose Steiner stir in her sleep, and turn her bulky form sideways, and observe Otto Steiner staring up at the ceiling, just as Gladys Turner was doing. The light was out, and only the moon shining through the windows showed her the pale face of her tubby husband, his eyes wide open.

'Otto, *liebling*, you are not sleeping. Come now, close your eyes and rest. All will be well.'

Otto Steiner had slept badly ever since the Hamburg days, and there was the thing that was always with them by day and by night, and she thought it was that which was worrying him. Therefore she spoke to him soothingly, and reached out with her hand beneath the bedclothes, and grasped his.

Otto Steiner had been a man of strong nerves until the Brownshirts broke his spirit; now he was a man who panicked easily. Afraid of his own shadow, some said.

Obediently, he closed his eyes, till he heard Rose's regular breathing. Then he opened them again.

Not an attractive couple, really. Both of them fat. She with her dyed yellow hair, and he with his fringe of grey hair round his bald head. Nevertheless, made of flesh and blood, the same as anybody else, and filled with hopes and fears, too, like others.

But in Otto's case, more fears than hopes.

Useless to linger over the Steiners, that bespectacled German-Jewish couple. When the flames die down at Number 127, they will be among the ashes for a certainty, groping about in their short-sighted fashion, muddling around trying to stumble out through the ruins.

Not much good at that sort of thing, are you, Otto? Not these days.

But a glance, perhaps, at Rachel across the passage, in her first year as a doctor at a hospital for women; slim, dark, intelligent and sensitive Rachel. She is wondering whether it would be right to risk marriage with a *goy*, a non-Jew, even though they love each other. The outlook, the customs, the traditions, so different.

Poor Rachel, so clever professionally, so incapable of deciding this problem of her own. She may be singed, too, with any luck, when the candles have burnt their course.

What about P.C. Maitland? He's of interest. Look at him now, strolling along Paton Street in the summer moonlight. Only twenty-five years old, but a very important young man, though he doesn't know it yet.

He ought to be keen-eyed and vigilant. Alert, on his toes, eager for promotion, concentrating on his job. But he isn't. No, indeed. He's not thinking about crime, he's thinking about his forthcoming annual leave, and what he and his girl friend will be doing, on a moonlit night like this down among the sand dunes in Devonshire, if he plays his cards right.

Meanwhile, Chief Detective Inspector Morgan sleeps on, though for him, too, the time is now running out. He hasn't much longer to lie there before the telephone rings at his bedside. P.C. Maitland may be in love, but he is not completely blind.

*

They wouldn't normally have got him out of bed at three-thirty in the morning, but arson cases are awkward. You don't want to lose time on arson cases.

They are tricky because evidence is almost always circumstantial, and circumstantial evidence must be iron-clad if a jury is to convict. Great care is needed by the police. Arson cases are not matters for young, inexperienced officers.

The guilty person usually makes arrangements to be well away from the scene before the fire is discovered. The fire brigade, inevitably, will have made a shambles of the place. Objects of use as evidence will have been moved or irretrievably lost before a suggestion of arson arises; containers, or crude delayed-action fuses, may have been mostly consumed in the fire or lost in the general clear-out when the fire has been subdued.

It was because of the latter possibility that Chief Inspector Morgan had given instructions that he was to be called at any hour of the day or night if arson was suspected. It was a standing order.

Gwen hardly stirred when he shook her shoulder, and murmured that he was going, and crept out of the house to his garage. Police officers' wives get used to such things.

So now he got out of his little car in Paton Street, and saw in the pre-dawn dusk the fire engines and the group of firemen. Some people returning late from a party had halted their car nearly opposite, and were idly watching; and the lights were on in a number of neighbouring houses. Pale blobs which were faces gazed out of the open windows, sometimes singly, sometimes three or more at the same window. But apart from two or three neighbours who had thrown coats over their nightwear there were no bystanders, for the hour was too early.

Inspector Morgan, in spite of the warmth of the previous evening, had put on a light overcoat, too, because a June dawn can be chilly in London, and now he thrust his hands into the pockets of the coat, and strode to the door of Number 127.

A broad, sturdy figure, Morgan, the breadth of his shoulders making him seem shorter than his five feet eleven inches. A bulky, aggressive figure, walking firmly, with short steps; head thrust forward, so that the chin seemed almost to rest upon the chest. And set on a short, thick neck, a granite, lined face; grey in the early light, inclined to be a little grey at the best of times; craggy, reminiscent of the Welsh mountain valley where he had been born. The eyes were grey, too; not big, not small, but rarely blinking, and restless, in the way detectives' eyes are.

Outwardly, a solid, bullish man. Inside, a mass of Celtic sensitiveness and intuition. A very deceptive man, Morgan.

Morgan stared at the building. He saw that the ground floor was a furniture and upholstery shop, the furniture still in the

9

windows, the glass panes of the windows intact. Above the shop, the windows had fallen out owing to the heat, and the shattered glass lay on the pavement.

The Inspector's footsteps rang out on the pavement, and the bystanders, and the police constable on the door, and the firemen at the tenders, they all turned round as he approached and stared at him.

The Inspector pushed past them and into the building, and climbed the narrow uncarpeted stairs; quickly, two at a time, in spite of his bulk; avoiding the trailing hoses.

Sergeant Shaw heard him coming up the stairs, and recognized the quick but heavy tread, and came out of the flat, past the green front door, the outside still unscorched, and met his superior officer.

'Nice bloody time to get up, Fred.'

'Yes, sir.'

Morgan had lost most of his Welsh intonation. Much of the lilt had been flattened out by twenty years' work in London. Only sometimes at home it came back. Sometimes at night, with his arm around Gwen, they would speak of the old days in the valley, and the deep softness, the inherited music, crept back along with the sweet pain of remembrance, and the nostalgia.

The Inspector stood in the doorway for a moment, and seemed to be listening. Sergeant Shaw said:

'The sitting-room is ahead. There are two small bedrooms on the right, sir. Kitchen on the left. Also the bathroom. Dining-room leads off the sitting-room.'

Morgan nodded, sniffling the acrid smell of burnt wood, burnt fabric, ashes sodden with water.

'Where's the occupier?'

Shaw shrugged his shoulders.

'Don't know yet, sir. The place was empty. They had to break their way in.'

'Who lives below? Anybody?'

Shaw shook his head.

'Nobody sleeps there. It's a furniture shop.'

'I saw that,' murmured Morgan drily.

'I've sent for the owner. He ought to be able to help.'

'Why do you think it's arson?'

Sergeant Shaw opened his notebook.

'I got a couple of statements after telephoning you, sir. P.C. Maitland – you saw him by the door on your way in – he says:

' "At about 1.50 am I was on my beat at the western end of Paton Street, when I observed a dull glow showing through the windows of the house I now know to be Number 127. At first I thought it might be the flames from a hearth fire, but in view of the warmth of the night I considered this unlikely.

' "A few seconds later, I observed flames at the windows, and assumed that the curtains were on fire. I knocked loudly upon the door which gives entrance to the side of the building, and obtaining no reply I forced my way in. I climbed the stairs, and saw that smoke was issuing from beneath the door of the flat above the shop.

' "In the circumstances, I considered it justifiable to force an entry, but almost at once was compelled to retreat by dense volumes of smoke. I shouted several times, but upon receiving no reply I closed the flat door to stop draught, and proceeded to the telephone kiosk at the corner of Paton Street, where I then summoned the fire brigade.

' "In my opinion, the flames increased with a speed and intensity which might indicate the deliberate use of an inflammable substance.

' "The occupier of the shop beneath the flat is known to me. He is a Mr Otto Steiner, and resides with his wife at No. 56 Risburgh Road, Hampstead. He and his wife attend the shop daily, where they are engaged upon the sale of furniture and the manufacture of upholstery, for which purposes they employ three young women at the rear of the sale room.

' "Mr Steiner and his wife came to this country from Germany as refugees from Nazi oppression in 1939. Mr Steiner was subsequently granted British nationality." '

Shaw looked up.

'Notice the bit about the speed with which the flames spread, sir? Now here's what one of the firemen found on entering the building.'

The Sergeant studied his notebook for a moment.

'I won't read it all, sir. What it boils down to is that he found the flat blazing fiercely in four different places, widely separated. That's a pretty sure sign, sir. There were flames in both the bedrooms, the living-room, and the dining-room. And clouds of smoke, but no actual flames in the corridors.'

Morgan nodded. He was only half listening. He was thinking that there was something wrong which at first he couldn't place, and it wasn't the fact that arson was suspected.

They were in the sitting-room now, standing among the ruins and the ashes and the smoke-begrimed walls, and the reek of it all was in his nose. But it didn't worry him, because you expect that at a fire. It was something else, a feeling in the spine which he recognized from the past.

Morgan would never have admitted to Shaw that he could smell death, new death. Shaw would have said:

'Yes, sir,' dutifully, and stared at him.

He began to move through the flat, stopping here and there to examine charred furniture, the thick hems of curtains which had not been entirely burnt, splintered floorboards dislodged by the firemen's axes. Once, near where the sitting-room curtains had hung, he knelt down and sniffed the remains of the wainscoting. When he stood up he said:

'Take samples of woodwork from the most charred parts of each room. And from chair and curtain fabric. Have it sent to the lab. You'll find traces of petrol all right. Soaked in. Some of it lingers, specially if they get the fire out quick enough. Only people don't know that. That's where some of these arson people go wrong.'

He hesitated, then added:

'Man, I've got an idea that this was a clumsy job. Have the ashes sifted, and keep an eye open for candle-grease, and wicks or string, or anything that could have been used as a fuse.'

He began to go through the flat again, room by room, opening the cupboards, opening drawers and shutting them again. Not knowing what he was seeking. Not knowing what was wrong. Only certain that something was wrong.

Cupboards and drawers held nothing of interest. There was

a little food in the kitchen. No letters or papers of a personal nature in the writing-desk. But in a glass ash-tray by the telephone in the bedroom a cigarette end with a pink smear on it, and the tobacco still in good condition, not dry from age.

Morgan picked it up, put it carefully in an envelope and gave it to Shaw. He said:

'Man, don't you feel it?'

'Feel what, sir?'

But Morgan shook his head. How talk to a man who was not brought up in the valley among folk who spoke about the Little People as naturally as Londoners speak about Frenchmen and Germans: they who came out of trees and hedgerows on moonlit nights, and feared iron, and could be spiteful or friendly? Morgan said lamely:

'There's something odd about this flat. I don't know what it is.'

'You'd think you'd find some letters, sir. Something personal, like.'

Morgan shook his head again. The Sergeant was wide of the mark. Miles wide of it. But you couldn't explain to Shaw, he so Anglo-Saxon and down-to-earth.

Vaguely he was aware that a car had stopped in the street, and shortly after he heard the tramp of feet in the shop below and the sound of voices. One of the voices was that of a woman, plaintive, loud.

'Not much doubt who that is,' said the Sergeant. 'Want to talk to them, sir?'

Morgan thought a moment.

'Not yet. Later perhaps, but not yet.'

He thrust his hands deep into his overcoat pocket again, and moved to the door of the sitting-room.

'Get a statement from them, Fred. Ask 'em who lives here, and so on. Make a few discreet inquiries. And you might as well try the inside front-door handle for fingerprints. Just in case. The outside handle, of course, will be smeared with P.C. Maitland's prints. Maybe nobody's touched the inside handle since the door was forced.'

He sighed, and looked once more round the sitting-room. It had been nicely furnished. Good-quality carpet, dark antique furniture, or late Victorian pieces of the more pleasing kind. A broad divan against one wall, upon which various coloured cushions had been arranged. Against another wall, a glass-fronted bookcase, and by the window an eighteenth-century writing-desk.

Everything was ruined now. Ruined and sad. The furniture half-burnt or badly charred, the glass melted from the front of the bookcase. The chintz and the cushions on the divan reduced to blackened desolation. Most of the paint burned from the walls, and two big arm-chairs now sodden wrecks. In some places the floor had been taken up so thoroughly by the firemen that you could see into the shop below.

Dirt and desolation. And cold and silence. Behind the noise of the tramping firemen, behind the distressed voices in the shop below, was the Silence which shouldn't have been there.

Chief Detective Inspector Dai Morgan suddenly felt his pulse quicken as he listened to the silence.

But you couldn't explain it to Sergeant Shaw, who wasn't Celtic, who would say he couldn't hear anything, not with that racket going on below.

'With petrol at four-and-sixpence a gallon, I reckon it must have been quite expensive getting this fire going,' said the Inspector, and left the flat, and drove home for a bath and some breakfast.

He told himself that this was going to prove one of the easiest arson cases he had ever investigated, and he didn't believe himself at all.

*

Sergeant Shaw came to him at four o'clock in the afternoon, and stood in front of his desk, and he had his notebook and some papers in his hand.

Morgan had been staring through his window, down into the street, thinking of nothing in particular, watching the people drag sluggishly by, all over-burdened with the heat of a sweltering June in London. He felt jaded himself, did not like hot weather, except in the mountains.

He had dozed in his chair for an hour after lunch, but un-easily, like a man who has set an alarm clock and even in his slumber is listening for the jarring ring of the bell. He looked at Shaw now, but without interest. The Sergeant was pleased with himself. You could see that. He had the expression of a man eager to impart interesting news. But it was not in this fashion that the bell would suddenly shrill.

'Well?'

'One or two interesting things, sir.'

'Such as?' said the Inspector dully.

He saw the eager light begin to die away in Shaw's eyes. This wouldn't do, this wouldn't do at all. He roused himself.

'Sorry, Sergeant. I'm beginning to feel the effects of getting up at three-thirty. What's the laboratory report say?'

'Analysis shows traces of petrol in the floorboards and wainscoting in the sitting-room and dining-room, in portions of two of the curtains and of one of the bed-covers. Also in parts of the upholstery of one of the arm-chairs and of the divan cover, sir.'

'Any idea of the method?'

'Can't say, sir. Nothing elaborate. Perhaps a few petrol-soaked rags. Candle-ends, or a bit of string as fuse. You know, the usual thing, sir. But we've found nothing conclusive yet, except that petrol and candles were used.'

'We knew most of that already. Anybody with half a nose could smell the petrol.'

It was not intended as a reflection on the progress which had been made. But Shaw muttered, 'Yes, sir,' and remained silent. Morgan looked up quickly.

Shaw, red-headed and quick-tempered, with the fair skin that goes with hair of that colour. His face flushed now, the mouth all buttoned up. Shaw, aged thirty-five, keen and ambitious for recognition, with a pretty, dark-haired wife, and she much made up with lipstick and mascara. You had to be careful with Shaw.

Touchy, was Shaw. Why?

Morgan glanced briefly out of the window again. He wondered about Shaw, more particularly about Shaw's wife. There is a high divorce rate among detectives. Detectives are out so much. Wives get lonely, find consolation. Maybe Shaw had to get on, or his wife would get out. Maybe that made him more touchy than most. You couldn't tell.

Gwen was different, of course. He was lucky there. He had a firm base to work from. A wave of tenderness swept over him when he thought of the way her eyes would light up with pleasure each time he told her that he was not working, that he would be home for supper, that they would spend the evening together.

Had Shaw a firm base to work from? He wondered.

Morgan had a disconcerting habit of commenting aloud on his own unspoken thoughts. He said now: 'We're not automatons, Sergeant. The public think we are, but we're not.'

Shaw moistened his lips, watched the Inspector wipe the perspiration from his forehead. He didn't know what the Inspector was talking about, but he had to say something.

'No, sir,' he replied obediently.

All anger had gone from Shaw now. It came quickly and it went quickly. He was disappointed by the Inspector's lethargy, but put it down to the heat. Morgan dragged himself more upright in his chair, pulled the chair closer to the desk.

'Anything else, Sergeant?'

'Yes, sir. Otto Steiner increased his insurance by £2,000 three months ago. The company, of which he and his wife are sole directors and shareholders, has been showing a trading loss for the past year, sir.'

He paused, began to look back through his notebook.

'I have the exact figures here, sir.'

'Never mind the figures. Anything else?'

'Well, the landlord of the Hand and Spear public house, at the corner of Paton Street, states that about five weeks ago he overheard Steiner talking business with another man, name unknown, and that Steiner was discussing the possibility of selling the shop and the contents and the goodwill of the business. Steiner was heard to say that he was contemplating going into the catering business, if he could dispose of his present business in a satisfactory way.'

'A fire would be as satisfactory a way as any. I told you this looked like a clumsy job to me.'

He was talking mechanically, trying to infuse some enthusiasm into his voice, to convince himself that everything was as it seemed, that he was dealing with a simple case of a naturalized foreigner trying to find a quick way out of his troubles. He stroked his chin, pretending to concentrate, to listen keenly as Shaw droned on.

'Inquiries in local garages, sir, have established that an individual of foreign birth answering to Steiner's description, driving a small blue car, number unknown, but resembling one owned by Steiner, purchased a two-gallon tin of petrol three days ago. The garage hand concerned remembers the incident because he went to some trouble to find, and wash out, an empty can, and did not receive what he considered an adequate tip for his trouble. Shows it doesn't pay to be mean, sir.'

'If he'd received a generous tip, he'd still have remembered.'

He imagined himself back in the flat again, among the desolation and the smell of burnt fabric and woodwork, looking at a cigarette-end with lipstick. He was hearing the protesting voices of the owners of the furniture shop, and the sound of the firemen's tramping feet, and the throbbing of the fire-tender's engine, and the murmur of the voices in the street.

Hearing the noises, but not listening to them.

Listening, instead, to the silence behind the noises. The unnatural silence which Shaw couldn't hear, even if it were pointed out to him; which, indeed, he would not dare to point out to Shaw. He pictured Shaw in the Scotland Yard canteen saying, 'Dai Morgan has started listening to silence, now!' Laughter, and the story slipping back to colleagues of his own rank, and perhaps to his superiors. Badinage, and behind the leg-pulling a hint that the Chief Detective Inspector had been over-working, was cracking up.

Therefore Morgan kept certain thoughts to himself, and always had done, telling neither Shaw nor anybody else that the dead radiate a silence which can be heard by some.

Cold and heavy it is, thought Morgan, the Welshman, and no comfort does it bring to those who can hear it.

Damage by water. Damage by falling debris, by loss of

trading facilities: to certain stock such things can be as disastrous as damage by fire.

No need, then, to set fire to the actual premises. The insurance money will be just as good, or almost, and the business can be closed without loss of face.

'As a method of defrauding the insurance people, it's a bit more subtle than the straightforward way,' said Morgan. 'Those who do it think they've invented something new.'

He sighed.

'There's not much new about crime, Sergeant. Somewhere in the records you'll find it's been done before. A few small variations here and there, maybe, but that's all. Yet they always think they are being original. You can almost hear them saying it: "Say, I've got a great idea for a fire!" or, "I bet I could kill somebody and get away with it – I've thought out the Perfect Murder." '

They drove back to Paton Street, later in the afternoon, the Inspector and the Sergeant in the back of the car, a uniformed driver at the wheel.

Nobody was hanging around the shop now. No constable was at the door. Some of the furniture was still in the window, but a handwritten notice on the door said: "Temporarily closed", though the door was not locked.

Inside, a representative of the insurance company, notebook in hand, was talking to a colleague.

The Inspector and the Sergeant passed through the shop, through to the little office at the back, where Steiner and his wife were waiting by appointment.

A third man was present, sitting at a desk, and did not bother to rise when the police officers came in.

'Mr and Mrs Steiner, sir. I don't know who the other one is,' Shaw added disapprovingly.

Steiner said hastily: 'This is Mr James Bleaker. He is our – he is the legal representative of the company. You will understand that in the circumstances, with much money to be claimed – '

His voice died away. A short, stout man, bald-headed, with a tonsure of grey hair. Brown eyes behind rimless spectacles. A slight accent, and speech which sounded as though he had a pebble in his mouth, soft and watery. Mrs Steiner reproved him gently.

'Ask the gentlemen to sit down, Otto!'

The Inspector looked at her. She was short, too, and almost as stout. Dyed yellow hair. A fur coat. Like her husband, she wore rimless spectacles. Unlike her husband, she made no attempt to disguise her watchfulness and suspicion.

Steiner drew two chairs forward.

'I do not think you need have worried about a lawyer, Mr Steiner. It's largely a matter of routine questions, at this stage.'

The man at the desk interrupted. He was about forty-five, dressed in ill-pressed striped trousers and black jacket, a stiff, butterfly collar, and a grey tie. A bony man, of medium height, with red face and hands, and soiled cuffs. His voice was unexpectedly high pitched.

'I have advised my clients that in view of their position as naturalized British subjects, and in view of the fact that in case of criminal convictions they may have their naturalization paper revoked, they should make no statement on paper without my advice. I trust that is clear?'

'Why are you worrying about criminal convictions?' said the Inspector coldly. 'Who said anything about crime?'

Steiner said quickly, in his liquid tones:

'It has been whispered that there are circumstances connected with the fire – '

'What circumstances?' asked Shaw.

Steiner shrugged his shoulders, smiled nervously.

'Let us say no more.'

'Why not? Why not say what you want?' asked Shaw loudly. Shaw regarded all foreigners as *ipso facto* rogues and scoundrels, and did not hesitate to show it. The Inspector said:

'It's your help we want, that's all. We only want you to assist us, sir.'

Steiner spread his hands and smiled again.

'See now, Mr Bleaker, all they want is my help!'

Bleaker lifted his head from contemplating a thumb-nail, and looked at the Inspector with his watery blue eyes.

'My clients will naturally help the police if they can. But

19

they will make no written statement at all except in my presence.'

'Nobody's asking them to,' said Shaw. 'Nobody has suggested a written statement, have they?'

'I wanted to make the point clear.'

Mrs Steiner, fidgeting with a diamond ring on her finger, said plaintively:

'We have to be careful in these things. We do not want trouble. We have had enough trouble. All we want is to do our business in peace.'

Morgan watched the diamond ring sliding backwards and forwards on her finger, backwards and forwards and round and round. He noted the anxious brown eyes, the perspiring face, the fur coat, worn to impress, despite the heat.

His heart sank. Two frightened people. A man and a woman to whom fear now came quickly, and so easily that they did not bother to try to hide it. People talked airily of fear, almost as though it was something to approve, because it offered a test to the soul. But too much fear robbed people of their dignity, endangered the moral fibres, bred evil, a desire to survive at all costs.

He was no automaton, that's what he had told Shaw. Sometimes he wished he was. Sometimes he hated the Welsh intuition which gave him a glimpse of things beneath the surface. Looking at the Steiners he thought of brown-shirted thugs. Shattered glass windows. The furniture thrown out on to the pavement. The idle crowd gathered round to watch. Kicks and blows. Flight and the new life, the new start. Doing quite well, specially after the war, when things were in short supply. Then not so well. Not so young any more, either. Temptation, the endeavour to be subtle: don't burn your own place, burn the place above. Claim damages from the insurance company, not for fire, but for damage by water and debris.

Not subtle, not even new. Just dreary.

Not an idle man trying to make money quickly, a crook by nature. Maybe some people can only fight so much. Then they begin to despair. They can't fight any more, they pack up, panic, take the easy way, which is finally the hard way. Aloud he said:

'Can you tell us anything about the occupier or occupiers of the flat above? We'd be very grateful if you could, sir.'

He could feel the atmosphere relax, the tension lessen.

Bleaker, the cheapjack lawyer, began examining his thumb again, long, bony wrists protruding from the sleeves of his jacket. Mrs Steiner stopped fiddling with her ring, and looked at her husband. Steiner said:

'Mr Hitchcock, he has the flat. But he is in the Foreign Ministry.'

'He's not living there now?'

'He has gone to Rome for two years.'

'With his wife,' said Mrs Steiner, helpfully.

'He has been away for a year and a half,' said Steiner in his liquid tones. 'Eighteen months, he has been away.'

'Did he let the flat in his absence?'

'Twice, he let the flat.'

'To whom?'

'The first time was for a year.'

He looked at his wife: 'What was the name, Rose?'

'Sylvester, a Mr and Mrs Sylvester. A very nice couple. Very friendly people.'

As she spoke, she nodded her head to emphasize her words. Nodded and smiled, eyes glinting behind her rimless spectacles. Seated on the edge of a hard chair, still in her fur coat, short fat legs protruding from beneath a tight-fitting skirt. Fleshy feet bulging out of black patent-leather shoes. The insteps of the feet dimpled with fat.

'And the second time?'

'For the last six months, a gentleman called Mr Robert Draper has had the place.'

'What's he like?'

Otto Steiner shrugged his shoulders, looked hesitatingly at his wife.

'What is Mr Draper like, Rose? How would you describe him?' But before she could answer, he said: 'We hardly ever see him. We understand he works in the City. He leaves before we come to the shop in the morning, and he comes back at night after we have closed.'

'Where is he now?'

'Away with friends perhaps?'

Morgan nodded. All this was of little value, but it had served its purpose, it had helped to break down the wall of resistance which he had sensed when he first came into the office.

The Sergeant had warned them that he was going to call on them. Both of them had been bristling with defensive hostility; keyed up for cross-questioning, alert, shrewd, prepared to defend to the end their liberty and livelihood. The barricades had been up in earnest, and to help in their defence was the lawyer James Bleaker.

Morgan could hear the footsteps of the insurance men above, moving methodically around. He prepared to edge cautiously closer to the questions he wanted answered: exactly when the insurance on the business had been increased, why Steiner had bought a two-gallon can of petrol, where the petrol was now, whether the occupant of the flat had left a spare key with Steiner, where Steiner had been on the night of the fire.

Suddenly he heard the footsteps of the insurance men descending the stairs, hurriedly, their shoes clattering on the linoleum, and his nerves began to tingle.

Long before the footsteps had entered the outer shop, before the knock sounded on the office door, the Chief Detective Inspector knew that this was the moment he had been waiting for. The alarm bell was ringing at last.

He got up hastily when the knock came, and opened the door, all lethargy gone now, expectant and eager, and looked at the pale face of the elder of the two men.

'Could we have a word with you, Inspector?'

He nodded, murmured a word of apology, and went out, closing the door behind him. When he was out of the office one of the men said, voice quavering:

'I think you'd better go upstairs; there's a dead bloke up there. In the divan. It's one of those divans which open up like a chest. He's –'

The man's voice choked. Morgan nodded.

'So that's where it was,' he murmured, and turned and opened the door, and called for Sergeant Shaw.

Chapter 2

BRILLIANT amateur detectives, when assisting the police, or when engaged in making the police look foolish, never make mistakes, and since brilliant amateur detectives don't exist there is no reason why they should. Chief Detective Inspector Morgan on the other hand made several mistakes in the Paton Street Case.

His favourite type of case involved confidence tricksters, for whose ingenuity and nerve he had a real admiration. Although they brought him publicity, he was not fond of murder cases.

Ministers of State, clergymen, children, old ladies, they all delight in murder because they don't see the result of it, because in books, thought Morgan, gazing down into the opened divan, the victim's injuries are neat and tidy. The clean bullet-hole in the temple, the tiny wound made with the thin Italian stiletto. Neat and tidy and glossed over quickly.

But in life there is mess, grotesque distortion, blood, discoloration, and all around the heavy leaden silence which is not of this world, which a few can hear and most can not.

That is murder.

It is also the catch in the throat, the feeling of nausea, which you cannot show because you must put on a business-like front before the younger detectives, the search of soiled clothes, the listing of the contents of pockets, the shaking out of dust from trouser turn-ups, the search for missing buttons, rents in garments, for signs of a struggle, and the examination of finger-nails and of hair.

It is also the examination of the wound in the hair, thought Morgan, bending down, peering at the wound at the base of the skull, with the heavy bruise, and the blood and the torn skin, and the fractured bone; peering at the body and the face, all blackened with the flames, like the inside of the divan, and most of the clothes burned from the body.

Most of the clothes were burnt, but not all, not the part of the jacket upon which the body was lying, in a reclining attitude, the knees partly bent. That part of the jacket would be unburnt, thought Morgan, and knew that he was mildly surprised that the victim was a man and not a woman.

He was annoyed with himself, feeling that he had been influenced by the cigarette butt with the lipstick smear, that he should not have been, that the cigarette butt might play no part at all in the matter. Unreasonably, illogically, he was glad that it was a man and not a woman, though a man has as much right to live as a woman, and more so, in some cases. Behind him, Shaw said:

'Can't understand why he was put in the divan. Why wasn't he left on the floor, in the chair, in the open? If the fire brigade hadn't got the flames out quickly, he'd have fallen through into the shop below when the floor gave way, with all the furniture and stuff. Been found among all the debris, and the wound could have been explained – or argued about, anyway. I don't get that.'

Morgan shook his head, said:

'You don't know, and you can't know, what goes on in a killer's mind when he's done the job. Maybe he thought there might be a long delay before somebody, sometime, opened the divan. Maybe he could use the delay. You don't know in these cases, Fred, you just don't know.'

'He was longer than the divan,' said Shaw. 'They shoved him in before rigor mortis set in, they were able to bend his knees. So it looks as if the job was done in the flat here, and not somewhere else and the body just dumped here.'

Morgan nodded. Shaw was inclined to state the obvious.

'Not that that gets us far,' added Shaw.

'No,' agreed Morgan.

He was thinking: they are nearly through now, with their cameras and flash-bulbs, and measurements and sketches. Then they will all go back, and there'll be the developing and printing and enlarging, big, expensive enlargements, and the drawings to scale; and later the pathologist's report, and his fee, and the experts hired; and the prosecuting counsel, and the judge, with luck; and his own time, and the other detectives' time, and all of it costing the money, including perhaps the hangman's fee. Chief Detective Inspector Morgan was Welsh, and that meant the warm impulse and the thrift; the instant generosity to the neighbour in trouble, but the general economy, the savings, the growing bank balance.

The thought of the public money spent on a murder case always appalled him.

They were packing up now, folding their equipment, putting their sketchbooks and notebooks in their pockets, murmuring together in subdued voices, for death is death, however many times you see it in your career.

They were going out now, the technicians, in ones and twos, out of the desolate flat and the ruin, through the green front door, and their feet were resounding on the uncarpeted stairway.

Downstairs was the man called Bleaker, and Otto Steiner, and Rose Steiner, waiting in the office for him to see them, and outside in the street were the police cars, and the ambulance, and the crowd, and again the constable on the door. Waiting with the constable was a small group of men eager for a statement, eager to telephone their news editors.

In the flat, there remained Morgan and Shaw, two fingerprint experts doing their best in difficult conditions, and two young detective constables.

'Okay?' said Sergeant Shaw, and Morgan nodded. Shaw said.

'Come on, you two – lend a hand.'

When they had lifted it out of the divan, and placed it on the floor in the light, Shaw said to one of the youngsters, who had coughed hurriedly, and was pale:

'You ought to have thought of this sort of thing before you joined the Force, Bailey. That's what you ought to have done. Too late now.'

He spoke blusteringly and loudly, partly to hide his own revulsion, to add a matter-of-fact air to the business. Morgan said:

'One of you – Bailey will do – sift through the ashes in the divan. See if there's anything there. Ferguson, you'd better take a list of stuff.'

Shaw was going through the contents of the right-hand jacket pocket, and handed a small diary to the Inspector. Morgan riffled through it quickly, said:

25

'It's pretty empty, except for a few names of horses and race meetings. It's one of those diaries bookmakers give you for Christmas, if you lose enough money to them.'

Bailey came over with a collection of things found in the divan. Shaw said:

'Right, Ferguson, take this lot down as I sing it out. Found in jacket: one bookmaker's diary, containing the name of R. Draper inside. One receipt for three ties from the Snowclean Dying & Cleaning Co, Notting Hill Gate, dated May 25th, made out to R. Draper, 127, Paton Street. One packet of cigarettes. One handkerchief marked Draper. Found in divan: a small pocket knife, seven and ninepence in coins, one propelling pencil.'

'What about his wrist-watch?' said Morgan.

Shaw removed it and examined it and said:

'Add to things found on body – one silver or nickel-plated wrist-watch with metal strap. Hands stopped at twenty minutes past twelve. Inscription on back: illegible. Pass to laboratory for treatment.'

Morgan went over to the window, stood looking down into the roadway, watching the small crowd, thinking. The evening sun glinted on the cream ambulance below, on the shining black bodywork of the police cars, on the red London Transport buses nosing their way past the end of Paton Street. The sky was blue. He was examining a theory and not liking it.

He thought that if Otto Steiner had killed Draper and fired the flat, his wife might know nothing of it, and in that case Rose Steiner was going to receive one more blow from Fate. He thought it strange how some people seemed to get all the kicks out of life, and some people all the gravy. He imagined Rose and Otto flying surreptitiously from Hamburg with their children. Leaving everything, cutting their losses.

And now, what now? Aloud, he said:

'Is the telephone still working?'

One of the detective constables said:

'Yes, sir. It's in the bedroom.'

'Get old Thompson to do the pathologist's report, Fred. Give him a ring now. Say the body is on the way. If he's too busy to take it on, get him to have a look at it and establish the time of death, as near as possible. It's probably somewhere about twelve-twenty, according to the watch, but you can't be sure. Also the cause of death. Say I want those in an hour or two. He can hand the rest of the job over to somebody else, if he wants to.'

'Yes, sir.'

The Sergeant began to move to the door.

'And Fred?'

'Yes, sir?'

'Don't take no for an answer. You know what the old boy's like. Tell him it's important, and the whole bloody police force is relying on him. Flatter him.'

'I will, sir.'

'And Fred?'

'Yes, sir?'

'You see the alternatives, up to now?'

Shaw hesitated, wanting to put his views forward, wanting recognition, but finding his views difficult to express. Unwilling to stumble and flounder, he hesitated. Morgan, sensing the reason, said:

'Perhaps whoever decided to set the flat on fire only discovered the body at the last moment, when all the other preparations were finished. Maybe he thought he would find some clothes or other inflammable stuff in the divan, something to help with the fire, and found a body instead. Nasty shock for a man, that.'

'If it was a man, sir.'

'On a pure arson theory, it probably was. Women don't go in for arson much. Even pyromaniacs are rare among women.'

Morgan paused, added:

'So then what?'

'So then he panicked, sir.'

'Yes,' said Morgan, and after a few seconds he said, 'Yes' again, and added: 'But I don't think so.'

'Neither do I, sir.'

'Or maybe it was a carefully planned murder? Maybe he set the scene, and when Draper returned, he killed him deliberately, and set the fire going, and left.'

27

'Maybe.'

'What's your theory?'

'Same as yours, I expect, sir. Somebody wanted to burn the place down, and got disturbed by this chap Draper.'

'Therefore somebody who knew Draper?'

'Yes, sir. Somebody who thought he knew when Draper was going to be out. Only he was wrong. Unfortunately for Draper.'

The Inspector nodded, took out his old, mended pouch and began to fill his pipe.

'All right, Sergeant, tell the ambulance men they can come up and take this poor bloke away.'

'Yes, sir. And I'll give the wife a tinkle, if I may. Just to say I'm going to be late.'

'Of course, Fred.'

A casual request, casually granted. Everybody knew the Sergeant was on a leading rein on the home front. Shaw knew that everybody knew it. It was never referred to, of course. The pretence kept up, thought the Inspector, the dignity preserved.

In the valley it was the respectability, the good name among the neighbours, the ability to entertain the visiting minister as well as the next man. In Shaw's case, the pretending that all was well in his home, when everybody knew that Ena Shaw was a fly-by-night.

In his occasional moods of Celtic depression, the Inspector saw Shaw in the dock. Shaw, with his red hair and quick temper, and his love of a flighty woman, the love that might make him kill her, and he answering guilty to the charge, and making no appeal for mercy; only longing to join her wherever she might be. But usually the Inspector was too busy for such thoughts.

Only sometimes, when the love he had for Gwen, and she had for him, made him silently count the years they might hope to be together, he would compare his own happiness with the ill-fortune of others.

So now he passed his hand over his greying hair, and said:

'While you're at the phone, Fred, you might give mine a buzz, too, and tell her the same.'

Shaw was pleased, as Morgan knew he would be: the Inspector – he, too, had to ring his wife.

The Inspector went downstairs and into the narrow hallway, and as he turned left to go into the shop one of the newspapermen shouted:

'Anything for us, Inspector?'

He shook his head, called back:

'You know about as much as I do, at the moment.'

It was nearly true. What did he know of Robert Draper? At present, the man was merely a name and a charred corpse.

He went through the shop into the little office. Nobody got up this time. Otto Steiner at his desk; Bleaker, the lawyer, on a chair by Steiner's side; Rose Steiner now sitting at the table where Bleaker had been before.

Steiner with the bald head, and the fringe of hair, and the liquid brown eyes behind the rimless spectacles, watched him, openly anxious, as he closed the office door. Pale. No actor, Steiner. A frightened man. But a man whom life had frightened. You had to remember that.

Dumpy Rose Steiner, grey eyes glittering, she watched him, too. Still wearing her fur coat. Mouth compressed into a tight line. No anxiety here, only suspicion, defensiveness, hostility. Ever ready to see persecution in a new form. Ever ready to attack or retreat, but mostly to retreat; subtle and elastic in mind; of the blood that has eaten the bread of affliction over the centuries, the ear alert for the howl of the distant mob, for the battering on the ghetto doors by night, the eye and the brain vigilant to read the signs of the approaching pogrom.

Otto Steiner spoke first, moistening his lips with his tongue:

'It is terrible, this news. Anything we can do to help –'

His voice died away. He swallowed, shrugged, fumbled for a cigarette.

James Bleaker cleared his throat, and said:

'My clients will do anything in their power to assist, Inspector.'

'That's what I understood Mr Steiner to say,' replied Morgan acidly.

Morgan had no intention of interrogating them at the moment. You have to have all your ammunition assembled for a hostile interrogation. So far, he had too little. For the present, he sought cooperation.

'I want to know all that you can tell me about this man Draper, Mr Steiner. I want to try to build up a picture of his life. I would like to know something of his past, of his job, of his friends, and whether you know of anybody who harboured a grudge against him.'

Steiner nodded. Rose Steiner sat watchful and alert. Bleaker had his eyes fixed on Steiner.

'Where shall we start?' asked Steiner in his watery voice.

'He was, I believe, an acquaintance of yours?'

Steiner glanced at Bleaker. Through the smoke from his pipe, beyond the brightness of the flame as he applied the match to the pipe-bowl, Morgan saw a glance; fleeting and transient, little more than a movement of the eyelids. When Morgan had blown out his match, Bleaker had looked down again and was once more examining his thumb nail. Otto Steiner said:

'No, I did not know him. Just once or twice I saw him, when he was moving in. Otherwise, he had always gone when we arrived. And he came home after we closed. Like I said, Inspector.'

'I see.'

'Mr Sylvester, he satisfied himself that Mr Draper could pay the rent, of course,' said Mrs Steiner quickly.

'He told me he had references from Mr Draper's bank,' said Otto Steiner. 'Quite satisfactory, they were. I said to Mr Sylvester, "Mr Sylvester," I said, "I do not mind you subletting the place, if Mr Hitchcock does not mind, but you must get respectable people. I do not want trouble," I said.'

Mrs Steiner leaned forward, and said:

' "Go to the estate agents who sold us our lease, Mr Sylvester." That is what I told him. "Go there; they will find you a respectable tenant. Wainwright and Thorogood, in Kensington Church Street, very handy, too." '

'And he went there?'

Mrs Steiner nodded.

'He wrote to them. I know, because as we were closing one day he came down with the letter, and it was raining. So I said,

"We will post it for you, Mr Sylvester. Do not bother to go out in the rain," I said to him. "We will post it." That's right, is it not, Otto?'

'Yes, that is correct, Rose.'

'And the next morning, Mrs Sylvester, she came down and told me she had shown Mr Draper round the flat at about ten o'clock, only an hour or two after the letter must have arrived.

'Very quick letting, it was,' said Otto Steiner.

'Flats do not remain empty long now,' said Rose Steiner.

'One can get very good rents,' said Otto Steiner.

'But Mr Sylvester, he was not a greedy man,' said Rose Steiner.

'What rent did he ask?'

'Eight guineas a week, one quarter in advance,' replied Otto Steiner promptly. 'Very modest rent, considering.'

'Considering the beautiful furniture,' said Rose Steiner.

'And the state of the decorations. I think he could have got nine. Maybe ten,' said Otto Steiner.

'But Mrs Sylvester said he would rather take less and let the flat to a bachelor with no children or dogs.'

Morgan listened to the flood of words. The talk flowing easily now. No restraint, no hostility. The occasional shrug. But no mention of the fire, of course. What if he mentioned that? What then? But he had no intention of getting on to tricky ground yet.

'Where did Mr Draper work, Mr Steiner?'

'That Mr Sylvester did not tell me,' said Otto Steiner.

'Perhaps the house agents could tell you, perhaps they could help,' said Rose Steiner.

Bleaker was picking at a loose thread in the knee of his striped trousers. Bleaker stopped picking at the thread. He looked up at Mrs Steiner with his watery blue eyes, then down again.

Morgan saw it, and with his Celtic intuition he felt the atmosphere tighten again; but his mind was on the list of things found on the dead man. Running over it, item by item. Diary, cleaners' receipt, small change, pocket-knife, wrist-watch, propelling pencil.

It was wrong somewhere. All along he had known it was

wrong, but he had not been able to say precisely why. Now he knew, and the answer was so obvious that he was momentarily exasperated with himself and his assistants because nobody had spotted it.

They had been looking at what they found, considering what there was, examining objects, conjecturing about things which were present. They had omitted to think of what was not there, of what should have been there and was absent; forgetting that the absence of something could be as significant as the presence of something.

They had not asked themselves how the unfortunate Draper got into the flat, his own flat, without a latchkey, or if he had had a latchkey, where the key was now, or if he had not had a key, to what trusted person he may have said, 'You take the key, you'll probably get there before me.'

They were looking at him keenly now, not Bleaker, but the Steiners. The woman's eyes were watchful behind the rimless lenses, the man's showed once again the hint of fear. Semitic intuition, like Celtic, was highly developed.

On Otto Steiner's lips was the smile that indicates a desire to please, but in the eyes the apprehensive light. On Rose Steiner's lips, the smile that tries to deceive, but in the eyes the alert look of the cat which ponders which way it will have to jump.

Yet Morgan had said nothing. Only his expression must have changed, or the look in his eyes, or his lips may have tightened. Very little, but enough for the Steiners. He struck another match, and said:

'How many keys were there to the flat upstairs?'

'Two,' said Otto Steiner.

'Two for the flat, and two for the shop,' said Rose Steiner.

'Have there ever been any other keys?'

Otto Steiner shook his head.

'When we bought the lease of the premises, there were the two sets of keys only.'

'Has the lock ever been changed?'

'No, never. Nor have any keys been lost. Here are the two shop keys.'

He opened the door of his desk, took out two keys, held them up, as if to emphasize his words. He was happy again. So was Mrs Steiner. They were answering the questions about the keys quickly and willingly.

Suddenly Bleaker looked at his watch and said:

'Are you likely to detain my clients much longer, Inspector?'

'Who's detaining your clients, sir?'

'I have an appointment shortly, and I am sure Mr and Mrs Steiner wish to get home.'

'They are quite at liberty to leave, if they wish, sir.'

It stuck in his throat to call Bleaker 'sir'. The lawyer's behaviour puzzled him. He wondered whether he had imagined the exchange of glances between Otto Steiner and Bleaker, whether he had imagined, too, that Bleaker had shown interest when Rose Steiner had mentioned the house agents.

On a sudden impulse he got up and said:

'Well, Mr Bleaker's right. I mustn't take up much more of your time. I want to have a word with the Sergeant, and then there's a couple more questions I want to ask, and then we'll call it a day.'

Without waiting for a reply, he opened the door and went out. He knew they would wait for him. They would not be happy in their minds until they had heard what he wanted to ask. Rose Steiner would be curious, and Otto Steiner would be uneasy. And Bleaker, the lawyer? Morgan did not know about Bleaker. He only knew that for some reason Bleaker would not leave his clients alone with the police.

Shaw was coming down the stairs. Morgan said in a quiet voice:

'Get on the blower right away, Fred, and get two men to tail Bleaker when he leaves here. Till he gets to work tomorrow. Get on to the local station and say it's urgent, and they've got to be here in ten minutes. Tell them I'll detain Bleaker for a few seconds on the doorstep, so they can get a view of him. Tell them to drop anything they're on, but to ring the Yard in an hour and I'll arrange for reliefs to take over.'

Shaw nodded uncertainly.

'What about the Steiners, sir?'

'Oh, the Steiners!' said Morgan irritably. 'They can wait. There's plenty of time for the Steiners. Get cracking on this first. And when you've done that, get on to Wainwright and Thorogood, estate agents, local, find out if anybody's still there; it's only just after six. Say we want full details of the transaction of the sale of the lease of these premises to the Steiners, including the number of keys handed over.'

Shaw nodded, retraced his steps upstairs to the flat and to the telephone. Morgan went back to the office and said briskly: 'Now just a bit more about the keys. Did you hand over both keys to Mr Hitchcock, the original tenant, Mr Steiner?'

Otto Steiner nodded eagerly, glad of an easy question.

'Both keys I handed over. And Mr Hitchcock gave them to Mr Sylvester.'

'And do you happen to know if Mr Sylvester gave both keys to Mr Draper?'

Steiner hesitated, looked at his wife, cleared his throat.

'No,' said Steiner. 'No, he left one key with me.'

'Any reason?'

Steiner said: 'Well, he – ' then stopped, shrugged his shoulders, spread his hands. Mrs Steiner said quickly:

'Tell the Inspector, Otto. Poor Mr Draper is dead now.'

Steiner said:

'It's like this. Mrs Sylvester, she was very particular about her flat. Kept it all nice, see? And Mr Draper, well, he was a stranger, wasn't he? So Mr Sylvester said, "Mr Steiner, here's a spare key; just have a look round now and then, eh? When Mr Draper is out, just have a look round. See everything's in order, eh? You want a clean, respectable tenant, same as me, Mr Steiner. So have a look round, and if you don't like the look of things drop me a line." '

'That's all there was to it,' said Mrs Steiner. 'Just keeping an eye on the flat for Mr Sylvester, that's all.'

'Still got the key, sir?'

'Yes, I've got the key.'

He opened the drawer again, took out a Yale-type key.

'Mind if I keep it, sir?'

'Any particular reason?' asked Bleaker, suddenly.

'Yes,' said Chief Detective Inspector Morgan, and turned his square, lined face and grey eyes towards the lawyer. 'Yes, sir, there's a very good reason.'

'Are we permitted to know the reason?'

'You are, sir.'

Bleaker hesitated, suspecting a trap, not expecting ridicule. Morgan got up, said mildly:

'If we haven't got a key, we can't get into the flat once the door's shut. Can we? It's as simple as that. Satisfied, sir?'

He picked up his hat and gloves, and the black brief-case he carried with him on investigations, and looked round the little office.

On the mantelpiece were two enlarged snapshots, in cheap wooden frames. One of a girl of about twenty-nine or thirty, dark thick hair taken severely back from the forehead, wearing a simply cut coat and skirt, and standing on some front door steps with some books under her arm.

'That is our daughter,' said Otto Steiner, smiling. 'A very clever girl. One day she will be a famous doctor, I think. A Harley Street gynaecologist, drawing very nice fees!'

'And the other?' asked Morgan, looking at a family group of a young man with horn-rimmed spectacles, a dark-haired girl, and two small children.

'That is Julius, our son, with his wife and children,' said Mrs Steiner. 'They are on a picnic. It is taken in America.'

'Rachel lives with us at the moment,' said Otto Steiner, 'but our son, he went to America in 1939.' He stopped and shrugged. 'One could not tell what would happen if war came. We had a little money put by. For us, it did not much matter if the Nazis came here. Much of our life was over. But we thought it best to send the children.'

'I have a sister in America,' explained Mrs Steiner. 'We sent the children to her. Just to be sure, eh? Rachel, she came back after the war, but Julius, he stayed on. He is an American citizen now.'

'Doing well?'

Otto Steiner nodded, said slowly:

'Yes, he is doing very well. He has a very good job. A nice wife, too, I think, though we have not met her. And two little children. God has been very merciful to us, so far, Mr Morgan.'

'Yes,' sighed Rose Steiner, 'God has been merciful and kind.'

*

What of our celestial spirit now? Provided he is still off duty, he must be rocking with laughter.

There's Otto Steiner, for instance. Later that evening he's feeling much better. The flush of panic is over. He's had his first interview with the police, and things didn't go too badly at all, did they?

He's feeling pretty confident. He doesn't know that the finger-print boys got his prints off the inner door-plate of the flat door, and it was easy to get another set from the shop below. How could he know? Well, he'll know soon enough.

Of course, there's still the other matter which has been such a torment to him and to Rose for so long now, but he's almost got used to that. He thinks he's nearly out of the wood.

Even Gladys Turner is feeling better after her ghastly night.

She knows she's in a tricky position, of course. And Robert's death was dreadful, and all that. But Robert had let her down badly, and though she wouldn't say that a just fate had struck him down – no, no, nothing like that – yet it was rather a judgement on him, wasn't it?

All she had to do now was to keep her head and make a few inquiries. Everybody knew there were broadminded doctors about, willing to take a sympathetic view about certain things. Come to think of it, her own doctor might help.

She's a simple girl, Gladys.

She doesn't know that though she was in a bad spot before, she's in a far worse one now. Lucky Gladys. Make use of the breathing space, charge up your batteries, because that's the way it often goes in these cases: first, the panic about a minor situation, then the recovery, the feeling that things aren't so bad. And then the avalanche.

*

After leaving the Steiners and Bleaker, Morgan returned to the Yard and took the lift up to his room, and walked along the blue-grey corridor and found a brief history of the Steiners on his desk. Shaw must have telephoned the Yard on his own initiative and asked for the papers. That was where Shaw was so good. He uses his loaf, thought Morgan; in spite of his domestic worries, he uses his loaf. A bit slap-happy, sometimes: the blunt question, the bullying tone, when a more indirect approach is indicated, but a good man on a job. And he might mellow. In spite of his ginger hair and quick temper he might grow more mature, and then he'd go a long way.

Morgan sat down, refilled his pipe. He began to glance through the information, but the telephone rang, and he lifted the receiver.

'Shaw here, sir.'

'Where are you speaking from?'

'From Wainwright and Thorogood, sir.'

'Any luck?'

'Yes, sir. Mr Wainwright is with me now, sir. Shall I give you the dope now?'

Morgan drew a scribbling-block towards him.

'Go ahead.'

'A fifteen-year lease of the property at 127, Paton Street, comprising a two-storied building, consisting of shop premises and a flat, was sold to Mr Otto Steiner on September 4th, 1950, sir. Previous owners were the Kensington Freehold and Trading Company.'

'Who did the legal work?'

'Curtis and Curtis, of South Audley Street, for the Kensington people.'

'And for Steiner?'

'Our friend, sir.'

'Bleaker?'

'Yes, sir.'

'I see.'

Morgan hesitated, then said:

'Ask Mr Wainwright if he can say how many sets of keys were handed over.'

A pause, a distant murmur, then Shaw's voice again.

'Three, sir. Three keys for the shop and three for the flat. Sent to Mr Bleaker on completion of the sale on September 4th.'

'Is Mr Wainwright sure of that?'

'He's got a carbon copy of the letter, sir.'

'Steiner says he only received two. Two for the shop and two for the flat, Fred. Where do you think the others are?'

Shaw said cautiously:

'I see what you mean. A bit odd, sir.'

'If this chap Bleaker received three sets, and passed on two sets, what did he do with the others.'

'Maybe Mr Steiner was mistaken or not telling the truth.'

'I doubt it. Anyway, what about Draper, what reference did he give? We don't know anything about this bloody man yet, we don't even know who the next of kin is.'

'I've got a bit there,' said Shaw. 'He gave his bank in Perry Street, Bayswater, as a reference, and his employer, a Mr Edward Tilling, said to be managing director of Tilling and Ledcot, in the City.'

'Who the hell are they?'

'Big firm of bookmakers, sir.'

'I see. Anything else?'

'That's about the lot.'

'We'll have to start the house-to-house calls this evening, of course. Usual questions. Anybody see Draper go into 127, Paton Street yesterday evening? If so, what time? Was he alone? If not, who was with him? Anybody else seen to call? Description. Time. Any car seen outside? Description and time. Any unusual sounds heard? Anybody notice the flat lights on? Time. Anybody notice the fire before P.C. Maitland?'

'I think I know the form, sir,' said Shaw, with a tinge of irritation in his voice.

'All right, Fred. I'll be here for an hour or two, in case anything crops up. They've got it in the Stop Press of the evenings, so you never know. After that, I'll be at home. Right?'

'Right, sir.'

'Tomorrow, first thing, you'd better nip along and see this chap Tilling, and the manager of the bank. I'll come straight here and see if there's anything on Bleaker. 'Night, Fred.'

He replaced the receiver, and almost at once picked it up again as the bell rang. A woman's voice, prim and formal, said:

'Chief Detective Inspector David Morgan?'

'That's me.'

'This is Dr Algernon Thompson's secretary. One moment, please. Dr Thompson wishes to speak to you.'

Morgan held the receiver an inch from his ear, braced himself for the blast. A few seconds later a booming voice made the instrument tingle.

'Morgan, I will not – I repeat, I will *not* have you slinging these dead bodies at me out of the blue. I've got quite enough, more than enough – I repeat, more than enough – private work of my own, without the necessity to pick up a few guineas from you people. Is that clear? I say, is that clear?'

'Quite clear, doctor, but –'

'And another thing, Morgan, I will not, repeat *not*, have you putting time limits on things. "I want this in an hour, I want that in an hour." It won't do. I say, it won't do.'

'No, doctor.'

Algy Thompson blowing off again. Seventeen stone in weight, angry eyes and fringe of white hair, and the best pathologist available to the Yard.

'And you know damned well, Morgan, how difficult it is to say with certainty when a man was killed. You know that, don't you?'

'Yes, sir.'

'Got your pencil out?'

'I have, sir.'

'Well, take this down. You can have a written report in the morning. You're not having anything in writing tonight,' said the voice, rising to a sudden roar. 'You needn't think I'm keeping my secretary here all hours of the day and night to suit the whims of you people. Take this down.'

'Yes, sir.'

'Height, five foot nine inches. Approximate weight, twelve stone eight pounds. Aged about 38. Colour of hair, light brown, not bald, probably greying at sides. Got it?'

'I've got it, Dr Thompson.'

None of it was really what he wanted or what he had asked for. But Thompson did things in his own way. Finally it came out:

'Death occurred certainly within the last twenty-four hours, and certainly more than twelve hours ago. Probably between eighteen and twenty hours ago.'

'Cause of death, sir?'

'Partial fracture of the lower skull, by a blow at the top of the neck, followed by asphyxiation.'

'Asphyxiation caused by fire?'

'No trace of ashes or fumes in the lungs. But some particles of dust in the mouth, nose, and throat. Possibly a cushion or some such object was pressed over the face. Suggest you search the cushions in the room for traces of saliva.'

'Can't, sir. They're burnt.'

'Well, that's your affair. Can't help you any more. Report will be with you in the morning,' said Thompson brusquely, and rang off.

Morgan spent a few further minutes on the internal telephone organizing reliefs from the Yard for the local men who were following Bleaker. Although he acted at first on a hunch, he was now keener than ever to have the man tailed.

Why had Bleaker retained one set of keys, if he had? Morgan was uneasy about Bleaker, but not as uneasy as he was about Otto Steiner.

Morgan knew that nine murders out of ten are not deliberate. No planning has gone into them. That is why most of them are caught. Most killers blunder into the crime, not wishing to kill but to stun, to disable. One moment they are ordinary common little crooks, and then, in a moment of panic, they become murderers, the spotlight on them, the centre-piece of a drama in which they are totally unfitted to play the main role. They are insignificant in their lives, in all their crimes save one, in the dock, and even at the last dreadful moment of their earthly existence.

He looked at the information about the Steiners. It was a fairly common story. The Nazi oppression, the ruined business, the carefully organized flight to England, the fresh beginnings in a strange country.

But no Buchenwald, no Belsen, no Auschwitz with its gas chambers. Was that what Otto Steiner meant when he said that God had been merciful and kind to the family – so far?

Why had he added, 'so far'? Was it mere caution, or had he reason to fear that Divine protection might cease in the near future? Rose Steiner had echoed his words. But she had not added 'so far'.

Morgan shook his head impatiently. Speculation, all speculation. One had to keep to facts in crime investigation. First the facts, and then the theories. Fatal to seek the facts to fit the theories, selecting convenient facts, ignoring or belittling those that don't fit. But hard to avoid the theory, difficult to avoid the speculation. At what point was one entitled to begin to speculate?

He looked out of the window.

Storm over London soon. The heat not much abated, the air still and sticky, the collar clinging to the neck. The clouds banking up on the horizon, and they all blue and purple and yellow, and coming slowly nearer, and no stopping them.

Menace in the air. Like in a concentration camp before an execution. Before the hanging on the parade-ground in front of all the inmates.

Menace in the air, and justice to be done.

Otto Steiner, the German citizen, the family man, the respected trader. Otto Steiner, spat upon and buffeted and ruined. No Aryan blood, no State protection.

Otto Steiner, the British citizen. Trade bad, the insurance increased. The petrol purchased locally. Simple Otto, crude in crime? The first crime and all to lose? Disturbed by Draper? Panic, and the blow struck? Poor Draper!

Justice to be done, and he, Dai Morgan, from the valley, to see that it was done.

Home not so late after all, and supper and bed, and Gwen with her arm round him, and she saying:

'What is the matter, Dai, *bach*? Why do you shiver in this weather?'

Justice, but what was justice? The sin of the father visited upon the wife, upon the daughter with the fine career, upon the son in the good job, and the son's wife, and the son's sons?

Distant thunder, and the storm about to break.

41

Chapter 3

BUT there was no storm. A little thunder before midnight, a few drops of rain in the night, more thunder before dawn, and then the sun was out again; beating down on the white pavements, on rooftops and walls, so that by ten o'clock the rooms at Scotland Yard were already stuffy and overheated. Even the occasional movement of air from the nearby Thames was like a breath from a warm oven.

Chief Inspector Morgan had breakfasted off toast and coffee, and two aspirins for the headache which always swooped upon him at the slightest provocation.

His face looked greyer than usual, lined and grey, and he felt restless and depressed. The report on Bleaker's movements was not yet ready, but something else was on his desk, and on a sudden impulse he had himself put through on the telephone to Shaw, whom he guessed would be with Draper's bank manager.

Morgan said:

'I've had a report from the Information Room that a woman called Bellamy, of 138 Paton Street, wishes to see someone. I'll call myself. Pick me up there in about an hour, and I'll go with you to Tilling, the bookmaker.'

'Very well, sir.'

'Any luck?'

'It's difficult to say, sir. I'll tell you when I pick you up.' The Inspector glanced at a report on his writing-pad.

'And Sergeant?'

'Sir?'

'They've identified Steiner's finger-prints on the inside door-panel of the flat.'

'For certain, sir?'

'Quite certain. Excellent prints.'

He rang off. The discovery of the finger-prints was good news, of course – he told himself that firmly and repeatedly. If Steiner was the murderer, then Steiner had to be caught and hanged, and the finger-prints were a step in the right direction. In the end, he managed to convince himself that he was glad the finger-print department had done such a good job.

A knock at the door, and Algy Thompson's post mortem report. It appeared to add little or nothing to what Thompson had already told him the previous evening.

He wished the report on Bleaker's movements would come through, but kept his hand off the telephone, and went down to his car.

Number 138, Paton Street, in its Victorian heyday, had been of the pretentious pillared variety of houses, which are still to be found infesting Notting Hill Gate and Bayswater with their air of long-departed gentility. The tall pillars on each side of the front doors are mostly chipped and in need of paint. Inside, the floor-boards and doors and windows no longer fit closely, and groan and rattle beneath the pressure of feet or the impact of the wind. The ceilings are tall and ornate, and in winter the inhabitants are hard put to it to maintain some semblance of warmth. On the landings you will usually find windows consisting of small leaded panes of coloured glass, while at the back of the houses lie patches of dank grass, sour earth, and dark-leafed shrubs and sycamore trees, birdless and cat-haunted.

Paton Street has changed its character with the years, but four houses of this variety still survive, of which Number 138 is one, divided into what have come to be known as one-room flatlets, but which in more honest times were called bed-sitters. The larger rooms have a cupboard recess known, again in the modern jargon, as a kitchenette, while the smaller rooms are fitted with a gas-ring, which is still known as such.

Inspector Morgan tugged at an iron bell-pull, and heard a bell jangle somewhere in the depths of the building. After waiting for two or three minutes, he rang again, and heard footsteps approaching. The door was opened by a hard-faced woman of about sixty, wearing a dirty apron over a brown woollen dress.

'I am a police officer,' said Morgan, 'and I would like to speak to a Miss Elizabeth Bellamy, if she is in.'

The woman hesitated, then opened the door wider.

'Is she expecting you?'

'She suggested that I should call, but she gave no time. Is she in?' asked Morgan again.

'Oh, yes, she's in all right.'

The woman smiled, not pleasantly, but as though sardonically amused both by the question and her reply.

'Well, I suppose it's all right. Fourth floor. Door on the right,' she added, and moved off down the passage to the stairs which led to the basement.

Morgan climbed the linoleum-covered stairs to the fourth floor and knocked on the door on the right, and entered.

At first he thought the room was empty, and gazed around in astonishment. Heavy Victorian furniture. Rocking-chair and antimacassar. Small lethargic canary in a large ornate cage. Wax pears and grapes under a glass cover. A stuffed humming-bird, suspended by a wire, perpetually poised above a luxuriant wax flower, also protected by a glass cover, and placed upon a round table. The table covered by a dark-red cloth, the cloth fringed with tassels. On one wall a painting, brown with age, of wild cattle on a moor. On another wall some Zulu assegais, fanned out behind a Zulu shield.

Outside were streamlined cars, jet-planes, the hydrogen bomb.

'Come in, officer. I'm quite decently clad, I assure you. I saw your car arrive.'

The voice gave him a shock. He had been so intent on looking at the furnishings, that he had not noticed that the room curved round to the left, behind the line of the door. He turned in the direction of the voice.

Pushed directly against the window, so that the occupant could look out on to the street, was a large old-fashioned bed. Round the head of the bed stood a tall, painted wooden screen.

The Inspector estimated that Miss Elizabeth Bellamy must be over eighty years of age. The hand she extended to him was all skin and bone, but the grip was firm, so that the impression he had was of shaking the claw of a giant parrot.

She was sitting up in bed, wearing a pink bed-wrap. Tied into her hair were two pink bows to match. Her nose was

44

prominent and curved, her eyes small, blue, and surprisingly bright.

'Bring up a chair,' she said. 'Or sit on the bed, whichever you like.'

Her voice was steady, though it had the cracked timbre of old age, and she spoke in short, rather abrupt sentences.

'I hope you are not ill,' said Morgan feebly.

'Ill?' said Miss Bellamy in surprise. 'Not at all ill. Bedridden, that's all. Bedridden for donkey's years. Can't be helped. Things sent to try us, what? Affliction of the joints. All got to have something.'

On the window-sill by the bed were some modern detective stories. A pair of binoculars. Newspapers. A framed photograph of a young man with a large moustache. A packet of cigarettes. Two small pots containing cacti. Morgan eyed the detective stories with misgivings.

She followed the line of his gaze. She was as bright as a button. She said sharply:

'You don't need to listen if you think I imagine things. Never have romanticized. Don't intend to start now.'

He was reassured by the way she picked him up. He said hastily:

'You misunderstood me, Miss Bellamy. We're very grateful to you for getting in touch with us.'

She nodded and pointed to a newspaper.

'Been a murder at Number 127 – right? Suppose you think I imagine I can solve the crime. Don't imagine any such thing. But I thought you might like the description of a man who left the building last night. Not Steiner; I know him. Jew. Owns the shop. Not the other man. Different man. Never seen him before. Called there, stayed two or three minutes, came out again. He was accompanied by another man.'

The Inspector leaned forward eagerly.

'What time would that be, madam?'

'About nine-thirty, as far as I remember.'

She pointed to the binoculars, and said:

'I use those a good deal. They are a great comfort to me. I have got to know quite a number of local people. Visually, I mean. Some of them are almost old friends.'

45

She was talking more slowly now, less jerkily. He thought her earlier abruptness was probably caused by nervousness in the presence of a stranger. He doubted if she had many visitors. He guessed she was one of those people who live in the social waste land of the very lonely, a dismal area found in every town in the world.

'Do you think you could describe this man, Miss Bellamy?'

'Roughly. But you will realize that I did not pay much attention. There was no reason why I should. I jotted a description down after telephoning Scotland Yard. I have it here somewhere.'

She began to search among some pieces of paper on the window-sill.

Morgan thought: sometimes a man will go into the waste land out of charity, and bring simulated friendship, and after an hour or two return to the sunshine, feeling righteous but depressed; vowing he will pay another visit shortly; yet not going, for time passes quickly in the sunshine, and a man does not like to be depressed. And sometimes one of the denizens of the waste land will creep out from the shadows bearing a story which he will hawk round, hoping to be taken notice of. He is usually described as a liar, which indeed he often is. And he returns to the shadows.

'Here it is,' said Miss Bellamy, and the Inspector looked up. Was Miss Bellamy creeping forth from the shadows? Somehow he doubted it. He wrote down the details. Age? Couldn't tell. Perhaps thirty, perhaps forty. Not old, anyway. Height? About five foot eight or nine. Medium build. Not fat, not thin. Clothes? Grey suit; light grey, trilby style hat. Car? No, on foot. Any other details? No. The other man? Dressed in brown. Didn't notice anything else.

Morgan rose to his feet. He thanked her for her information. He said it might be very important indeed. He was, he repeated, most grateful. As he turned to go, he pointed to the photograph of the young man with the large moustaches.

'Who's the young man?' he asked politely.

'Oh, Charles,' replied Miss Bellamy, and smiled. 'He's my fiancé. They didn't want us to get married, you know, so they said he was killed at Ladysmith, in the Boer War. But I knew

46

they were wrong. He's learning to be a stock-broker. He advises me about my shares.'

She groped among some things on the table by her bed, found a small notebook, and consulted it.

'I made seven thousand pounds last year, thanks to Charles.'

'That's a lot of money,' replied Morgan evenly.

'He spends the evenings here, of course. And quite often comes here in the mornings. He's probably waiting for you to go, you know. He is rather shy about meeting strangers.'

Miss Bellamy indicated the room with her thin hand:

'I only keep the house on for him. He likes it. But it's too big, of course. Servants are such a problem these days.'

Morgan went downstairs in a thoughtful mood. He saw the woman who had let him in standing in the hall. She watched him as he came down the stairs.

'Does she own this house?' he asked quietly.

'Own it? She hasn't got two ha'pence to rub together,' said the woman scornfully. 'Own it, indeed! I like that! Last week she had rented it for the summer, the week before she had it on a five-year lease, and now she owns it, does she? That's good, that is, that's rich! Did she tell you about Charles, too? You don't want to take no notice of her!'

As he closed the front door behind him, he heard her cackling laughter echoing through the gloomy hall.

It was a happy start to the day's work.

*

In the back of the car with Shaw, the Sergeant said:

'The manager told me this fellow Draper had had an account with them for about six months. He transferred his account to them from the South Kensington Branch of the Scottish Union Bank. Not very much, about two hundred pounds. Apart from that, he didn't know an awful lot.'

'We'd better get on to the Scottish Union Bank.'

Shaw shook his head, and said:

'The manager did that off his own bat, while I was with him. It seems that Draper had been with the Scottish Union for about eighteen months. They didn't know much about him either, except that he was employed by Tilling and Ledcot.'

'Nothing else?'

'Only that Draper opened his account with five hundred pounds in one-pound notes.'

'Five hundred pounds in one-pound notes?'

'Yes, sir.'

'That's a bit odd.'

'That's what I thought. Still, people do funny things, sir.' Morgan was looking out of the car window, noting the river craft and the graceful spans of Waterloo Bridge, enjoying the ride because the movement of the car caused a pleasant breeze. He would have liked the journey to have lasted longer. His headache had gone and he was feeling well. And wondering about the five hundred pounds. Feeling that the money had some significance, but being unable to say why. Vaguely intrigued by it. Five hundred pounds. One-pound notes. And the transfer from one bank to another. Why the transfer? Was it because a simple transfer order from one bank to another would show no evidence of how the account was opened? And the manager at the Notting Hill Gate bank would have no occasion to think anything odd about Mr Draper? Suddenly he turned to Shaw and said:

'Have you had Draper looked up in the Criminal Record Office?'

'Nothing against him at all,' replied Shaw.

'That'd be asking too much,' muttered Morgan. 'What was the state of his account when he was killed?'

'Just in credit, sir.'

Shaw felt in his pocket, pulled out some papers, and said:

'The manager lent me his bank statements for the past six months, sir.'

Morgan took them, glanced through them as the car reached Blackfriars Bridge, crossed the traffic lights, and made its way up Queen Victoria Street. Cheques to Sylvester, to one or two firms which he recognised as bookmakers, to local traders. Credit payments from Tilling and Ledcot. Morgan said:

'One thing that annoys me is this – or maybe you can guess?' Shaw said:

'There's a lot of things that annoy me, sir, and most of them aren't connected with this case. In fact,' added Shaw with warmth, 'there's so many bloody things that annoy me that if I were to list them it'd look like the prelude to a hire-purchase agreement.'

Morgan laughed, then said:

'What annoys me at this moment is that we're having to treat this chap Draper as though he were a criminal instead of a victim. Chasing all round London trying to find out something about him, whereas if he'd only left his affairs nicely documented and in order, we'd know where we are, see? The people whom I like, Fred, are the nice orderly victims, living in a circle where all their friends and relations can rush forward with helpful information about them. I don't like these odd people who live their own lives.'

'They cause a lot of trouble, sir.'

Morgan began brooding about what a pity it was that the old war-time Identity Cards had been abandoned. With an Identity Card you had something to start on. It might be a false card, but even that had a kind of negative value. He was still brooding about Identity Cards and their uses when the car pulled up outside the offices of Tilling and Ledcot.

Mr Edgar Tilling was clearly intrigued to be face to face with two Scotland Yard detectives. He rose from his vast mahogany table with its glass top and battery of telephones while Inspector Morgan and Sergeant Shaw advanced across the luxurious thick-piled blue carpet. He held out his hand to each in turn and said in a North-Country accent:

'Sit down, gentlemen, sit down. What about a drop of Scotch?'

When they refused, he offered them cigars out of a large cedarwood box, and seemed surprised when they declined these, too.

There had been a time, when Mr Tilling was a young man in Manchester, when he and the police had not always seen eye to eye. There had been occasional trouble with street betting, a periodic fine, and a certain amount of intermittent hard feeling, at least on Mr Tilling's side. But it was all long ago. Ages and ages ago, it seemed to Mr Tilling. Almost as though it was a different life and a different person.

Now he wore expensive, Savile Row suits, and silk shirts, and his son went to Eton. And honest Ed Tilling, whose motto had been 'Safe and Civil', had made the grade. Honest Ed he had been, and bluff Ed he tried to remain. His firm was always courteous, even to the smallest punter, the humblest bank clerk, the typist with half-a-crown to gamble, because, as he regularly pointed out to his staff, the little sucker of today might be the big sucker of tomorrow.

Here and there among the small fry somebody was going to inherit money, or make money himself, or marry money, or have a friend or friends who might inherit, make, or marry money. And then who better to turn to in their palmy days than honest, bluff Ed, who subscribed heavily to the Conservative Party but also had a stake on the Labour Party?

So now Mr Tilling, after a suitable expression of horror at the sad fate of his employee, said:

'He was a queer sort of chap, Draper.'

'Why queer?' asked Morgan.

'Bit of a rolling stone, I gathered. Never opened up much about his past life. Still, he was all right at figures, and didn't try and fiddle the books, so he suited me. Got to take a man as you find him, you know.'

'That's reasonable,' said Morgan, and thought: shrewd, of course, shrewd as the devil – heavily built, red-faced, round-faced, shiny-faced, and about fifty-five years of age; that's Tilling.

'I always say that. Take a man as you find him, I say. Mind you, he got on with women all right. He was one of those soft-eyed guys with putty-coloured faces and a way of listening intently when women nattered to him. That's the way to get on with women, of course. Listen to them. If you want to get on with them, that is. Listen to them, pretend to be interested, even if you're bored stiff. Don't tell them about yourself, about how smart you are, about what some guy said to you and the snappy reply you gave.'

Ed Tilling drew on his cigar and said:

'Of course, if they're interested in *you* in the first place, you can talk your dam' head off, and they'll play the same trick, but the other way round, see? They'll do the listening, see?

And that's all right, that's fine. But if they're not interested, and you are, you got to do the listening, see?

'Still, I was a bit surprised poor old Draper got away with it so much.'

'Did he?' asked Morgan.

'Oh, I understand he was a bit of a one for the women,' answered Tilling and added: '*De mortuis*, of course, as the saying goes; still, there's no harm in a bit of fun now and then, if you get me.'

'Where did he find his fun?'

'Oh, here and there,' said Tilling, heavily vague. 'Here and there – so I'm told.'

Morgan said:

'Can you tell me of anybody in particular?'

Tilling leant back in his chair, and the chair creaked under his weight. The bluff, hearty exterior, the jovial air, and the home-philosopher manner, thought Morgan, but behind the hard blue eyes the calculating mind, the ruthless soul.

'What's the idea?' asked Tilling.

'I beg your pardon?' said Chief Detective Inspector Morgan coldly.

'There's no idea,' said Sergeant Shaw loudly. 'We're just asking you to help us, that's all. It's the duty of every citizen to – '

Ginger-headed Shaw at it again. Impetuous, quick to take offence. Morgan interrupted quickly:

'These are perfectly normal inquiries, sir, in a case like this.'

'This poor bastard's dead,' said Tilling. 'What's the idea of muck-raking around, eh?'

'Nobody seems to know much about Mr Draper. We thought you might help, that's all. Probably you can't.'

'I can,' said Tilling. 'If I want to, if I think it necessary.'

'But you won't?'

Morgan got to his feet, picked up his brief-case, added mildly: 'Well, it's a pity you won't cooperate, sir. I should have thought – '

'I didn't say I wouldn't,' replied Tilling hastily.

Morgan sat down again, replaced his brief-case by the side of his chair, and said:

'I'm sorry, sir; I misunderstood you.'

'I'm always willing to help the police, see? You know that? Well, this Draper feller, two or three of the women in this office were pretty keen on him. I know that. I've seen them hanging around in his room. Turned 'em out, too. Told 'em to get on with their bloody jobs. But he only went out with one, or so I'm told.'

'What is her name, sir?'

'Gladys Turner, Miss Gladys Turner.'

'Address?'

'She lives in Ilford.'

'Where?'

'Lime Lane, number 45.'

'Do you know the addresses of all your staff off-hand, sir?'

'She's my secretary. Any reason why a man shouldn't know the address of his own secretary?'

Bluff Ed Tilling was no longer safe and civil. He was out to score points. Morgan sidestepped the question.

'Would she be the young lady I saw coming in?'

'She wouldn't.'

'Then perhaps I might have a few words with Miss Turner, sir. Just in case she can help.'

'You can if you go to her place, I suppose.'

'Is she ill?'

Tilling shrugged, said:

'Don't suppose so. Said she had a headache, and was feeling sick. Probably read about Draper in the papers.'

'Can you think of any enemies Mr Draper might have had, sir?'

'I know one or two bookies who wouldn't have minded seeing him break his blooming neck, if that's what you mean?'

'Bookies?'

'Small ones, people like Joe Parsons and Reg Brown, and so on. People he's been owing money to for some weeks.'

Tilling waved his hand at his office furnishings.

'You'd think he'd know better, seeing what being on the other side of the fence has brought this firm, wouldn't you? But some of 'em never learn, not the small-timers.'

'Was Mr Draper a small-timer?'

'How could he be anything else on what I paid him? Not that he was worth more than twelve quid a week, mark you. Just an unqualified accountant, see?'

'How long has he been with you?'

'He was with me two years. But he was under notice. He got killed the day before he was going to leave. Poor old Draper! If I'd known –'

'Sacked?'

Tilling shrugged, and said:

'I got a cousin who wants a job. You know how it is? Got to make room. Blood's thicker than water, as the saying is.'

'During the time he was with you, do you know if he ever made a bet, or was likely to have made a bet, which would bring him five hundred pounds?'

Tilling laughed.

'We'd have heard about it if he had! My God, we'd have heard about it! If he won even a fiver he interrupted the whole bloody office routine while he spread the news.'

'Is five hundred pounds the sort of sum a man might receive in cash by betting, Mr Tilling?'

Tilling hesitated, examined the end of his cigar, and said:

'He might. It's just possible.'

'But it's unlikely?'

'It's unlikely that a regular punter would receive a round sum like that. Not a regular punter betting regularly with one firm. Even if he had some dough on a horse at straight odds like ten to one, or fifty, or a hundred to one, there'd probably be odd pounds, shillings, and pence, credit or debit, outstanding on his account. Anyway, he'd normally be paid by cheque. Unless it was on the Course.'

'One last question,' said Morgan. 'About these small bookies, sir.'

'What about them?'

'Do they ever get – a bit rough with people who don't pay up?'

'They don't love 'em like brothers,' replied Tilling shortly.

'That wasn't the question, sir. Might somebody call on a man who didn't pay up and perhaps – well, go over him a bit, so to speak.'

'It could happen,' said Mr Tilling, after a pause, in a dreamy, reminiscing kind of voice. 'Yes, I reckon it could happen, Inspector.'

In the car on the way back to Scotland Yard Morgan suddenly said:

'No cash drawings.'

He tapped Draper's bank statements with his finger. When Shaw waited for him to go on, he said:

'Cheques to the Sylvesters, cheques to local traders, and so on – but no cash drawings.'

Shaw nodded, and said:

'So where did he get his spending money from?'

'And come to that, how did he afford to take a flat like that?'

'On twelve pounds a week, sir. Not to mention his women.'

'Woman, anyway.'

'Where there's one, there'll be others, sir. With a type of that kind. I've met 'em.'

One of them left a lipstick-stained cigarette-end behind? A woman scorned? But could a woman heave a man of over twelve stone into a divan? She might stun him with a sudden blow, thought Morgan, she might subsequently smother him, but could she get him into the divan? Morgan doubted it. Not alone. But if a man were helping her it would be easy.

'I want the lipstick muck on that cigarette analysed,' he said.

'I've already sent it to the lab,' said Shaw.

Morgan was thinking again how easy it is to miss, not what is there, but what *ought to be there* and is not. Draper had no key on him, when he should have done. Draper's bank statements showed no cash drawings, when they should have done. Draper was getting money from somewhere other than his firm. But from where? Not from investments, not from private income. Certainly not from horses.

From women? Draper, the soft-eyed, putty-faced charmer who had a fascination for women – and was paid by them?

Waterloo Bridge again, white in the sun, spreading its spans like a seagull's wings. The Houses of Parliament, and Scotland Yard again, the modern building gleaming pale beside the older building.

Draper living on the immoral earnings of women? Draper set up in the flat by a rich woman? Draper the gigolo-type? Draper philandering, found out by the rich woman, quarrelling, and the tempers rising, and the back turned for a second or two, and perhaps a metal reading lamp easy to hand? All traces carefully removed, except one, the cigarette in the ashtray, carelessly put there while a phone call was made.

Or Draper the debtor, and the bookmaker's toughs, the insults, the threats that went too far, and again the blow struck?

Or Steiner, lighting his fire, in need of money? Steiner not knowing of Draper's death? Not knowing what was in the divan – at first?

Or Steiner disturbed by Draper?

Steiner, Draper – Draper, Steiner. Always back to Steiner in the end. Morgan got out of the car and slammed the door behind him, as though trying to break the vicious circle of Steiner–Draper. He walked to his room endeavouring to remember the colour of Mrs Steiner's lipstick, and found on his desk the first of the anonymous letters.

It was crudely written in pencil, in block letters, and said:

WHAT ABOUT THE BLOKE WHO CALLED AT 127 PATON STREET AT 9.30?

The Inspector stared at it irritably. He had thought he could discount Miss Bellamy's evidence. Now he began to wonder.

Chapter 4

THE laboratory came on to the telephone as soon as Morgan was back in his room. Vercoe, an assistant, said:

'That cigarette end – afraid I can't help you much.'

'I hadn't really much hope,' replied Morgan.

'It's an ordinary popular brand, and so is the lipstick on it. You can buy lipsticks like that in every chemist's shop.'

'I see.'

'I'll be letting you have the details in writing later in the day. Thought you might like to know, meanwhile.'

'Thank you,' answered Morgan gloomily. He was unwilling to admit even to himself that he had secretly hoped for any good results. Vercoe laughed and said:

'Having given you the bad news, here are a couple of items to console you. The end which had been lit was severely crushed, and at the other end the tobacco was tightly compressed and the paper slightly disordered.'

'You mean she uses a cigarette-holder?'

'Almost certainly.'

'Why the hell should there be lipstick on it if she uses a holder?'

Vercoe adopted the careful tone of one telling an expert something he should have thought of already. He said:

'Well, of course, some people light a cigarette between their lips and then stick it into the holder. Especially if it's a long holder.'

'So you think she might use a long holder?'

'Not necessarily, but she might. And one more point – '

'What?'

'There was a small puncture about an inch and a quarter from the unlit end of the cigarette.'

'Made by what?'

'Possibly a pin.'

'To remove the end from the holder?'

Vercoe hesitated. Then he said again:

'Possibly, but I doubt it. Many holders have ejectors. Besides, a pin, or anything like that, is usually only employed when the cigarette has burned down almost to the end.'

'Any ideas?' asked Morgan.

'None. I'm merely reporting what I found. I'm not a detective.'

Morgan did not take up the challenge. Some days he might have done. He might have taken up the quick-fire badinage to which Vercoe was inviting him. But the report on Bleaker's movements the previous evening was now in front of him, and he was anxious to study it.

So he merely thanked Vercoe for ringing, and replaced the

56

receiver. He picked up the report and after the usual preamble read:

'Subject left Number 127, Paton Street at 6.20 pm and proceeded on foot to the juncture of Notting Hill Gate and Kensington Church Street, pausing once to buy an evening paper. He then entered the Greyhound tavern, where he bought a pint of beer and remained reading the paper until 7.5 pm, at which time he left the Greyhound and went on foot along Bayswater Road to the Three Stars tavern. He went inside, looked around as if expecting to see somebody, and came out and stood in the doorway. At approximately 7.15 pm he was joined by a woman, subsequently identified as a Miss Renate Brueckmann, German subject by birth. Description: aged about forty; height, five foot six inches; slender build, brown hair, grey eyes; straight nose, square jaw; heavily made-up complexion. She was dressed in a grey flannel coat and skirt and carried a pigskin handbag. It was noticed that both Brueckmann and Bleaker smoked continuously, the woman Brueckmann employing a holder for this purpose.

'The couple, who appeared to be on affectionate terms, remained drinking until about 8 pm, when they proceeded to a nearby restaurant and had a meal.

'Owing to the isolated tables chosen by subject and his companion it was not possible to overhear their conversation, but at one period they appeared to be engaged in a prolonged argument.

'At about 9.15 pm they left the restaurant and separated. I instructed Detective-constable Perry to follow subject, and he subsequently reported that subject had returned to his own residence, namely Number 34, Chalmers Court, Marylebone Road. I followed the woman Brueckmann.

'Brueckmann proceeded by Underground Railway to Hampstead Station, and thence on foot to Number 56, Risburgh Road, a small dwelling-house, where she remained about half-an-hour and then returned to Number 34, Chalmers Court.

'From discreet inquiries at Chalmers Court, I understand that Brueckmann is currently co-habiting with Bleaker. Number 56, Risburgh Road is occupied by Otto Steiner, a naturalized British subject, his wife Rose, and their daughter Rachel. Renate Brueckmann, born April 3rd, 1914, at Hamburg, came to this country on August 5th, 1952, to take up a post as translator and interpreter at the offices of the Rhine–Westphalia Travel Agency. At 8 am this morning, observation was again taken up at 34, Chalmers Court. At 8.20 am the woman Brueckmann was seen to leave, and proceeded by bus and Underground to her office in Regent Street. At 8.45 am Bleaker left, and proceeded direct to his business premises in Spring Street, W.2. Observation was then discontinued in both cases.

'Police records contain nothing to the detriment of the Steiner family, or of James Bleaker or Renate Brueckmann.'

Nothing to the detriment of any of them, thought Morgan. No chink of real light, but Renate Brueckmann, mistress of Bleaker, calling on the Steiners on the night after the fire. Alone. The long journey for the short talk. Alone. Without Bleaker, but clearly with Bleaker's knowledge. Renate from Hamburg, the Steiners from Hamburg.

What of it? thought Morgan irritably, and reached for the telephone directory. Otto Steiner was in the book all right. What was wrong with using the telephone? And again he thought: the long journey for the short talk. Why didn't she telephone? Why go all that way? And in the heat. Did she not care to trust the telephone? Why not? Or had Bleaker sent her to give some message with which he did not wish to be associated?

There was a perfunctory knock on the door and Sergeant Shaw came in. He said:

'There's a Mrs Wood downstairs. Says she wants to see somebody in connexion with the death of Draper, sir.'

'Where does she live?'

Shaw glanced at the slip of paper in his hand.

'She gives an Ilford address, sir.'

Morgan was anxious to snatch a quick sandwich, be on his way to see Miss Gladys Turner. Shaw, seeing him hesitate, said:

'Like me to see her first, sir?'

Morgan shook his head. If she was of no importance, he could hand her over to Shaw. If she was important, he could spare the time.

'Show her up, Fred. You never know.'

Shaw went out, closing the door behind him. Morgan waited, wondering. Busybodies, nosey-parkers, cranks, people wanting publicity, people keen to speak to detectives on a murder job, they'd all be along in due course. He glanced at a newspaper on his desk. There were pictures of the burnt premises, with a constable on the door, of himself and Shaw coming out the previous evening, and an enlarged snapshot of Draper which he had given for circulation to the Press.

He saw from the pictures of the premises that the Steiners were making the best of it. Large paper notices pasted across the windows announced in bold letters that a Great Sale of Damaged Goods was in progress. Prices were declared Ridiculously Low, because the stock had to be cleared.

He thought again of the people who would be rushing forward to give worthless or bogus information, of the house-to-house inquiries by his officers, of the impact upon the lives of people who thought their existence ordered and safe. If you threw a stone into a pond the resulting ripples were predictable, symmetrical, and in a little while the pond was as before. But in the case of a murder, the disturbance was more like that caused by a giant boot, remorselessly crashing its way through the insect world in a garden.

Some of the insects were crushed physically, others had their world destroyed or altered for all time; and others, the lucky ones, were mere onlookers of the catastrophe, viewing with indifference or morbid interest the hurrying and scurrying, the crash of other insects' worlds, the pain and the panic, the terror and the upheaval.

The police boot was collectively insensitive, as it had to be. It was powerful and crushing, and rightly so, inevitably so: heedless of what stood in its way, ruthless and implacable, it plunged on until it reached the end of the journey. Woe to the innocent, the unfortunate, the ones with something to hide, if the boot passed that way!

Footsteps in the corridor. Mrs Wood. What kind of insect? Lucky or unlucky, to be crushed or not to be crushed? The door opened and Shaw said:

'Come in, madam. Mrs Wood, sir.'

Chief Detective Inspector Morgan took one look at her and thought: she's crushed already, not by us, but some time ago.

The lines on the face that do not come quickly, slowly engraved over the years, the mouth drooping down, the furrows vertical on the forehead deepened by worry and grievances, the eyes querulous, bad-tempered. Forty-five, and shabbily dressed. Bad complexion, badly made-up, and the hair prematurely greying and none too tidy. Woollen stockings, not nylon which ladder and are uneconomic. The handbag large and well-worn, the shoes badly cracked and lacking polish.

A woman with a long story, eager to tell it; a woman to keep to the point if you had another engagement.

'Mrs Wood?'

A nod, and a tightening of the lips.

'Won't you sit down?'

On this chair? Yes, on that chair.

'Do you smoke?'

The drawer opened, the cigarette packet extended. No, she didn't smoke, hadn't smoked for years. Had given it up because she couldn't afford it. Didn't dare to start again. Not after all the trouble she had giving it up. She wouldn't go through all that again, no, she wouldn't.

Something to tell the police, some information to give which she thought might be useful? Yes, it might be useful or it might not. She couldn't tell. Perhaps the police knew it already? Probably they did, probably she was wasting their time. No, no, carry on, let's hear it. And in her own words.

The fervent silent prayer that her own words would not be too numerous.

'It's about Robert Draper.'

A feeling of irritation. Patience, patience. Speak gently, sympathetically.

'What about him, madam?'

'He was my husband, that's all.'

60

He was her husband, that was all! Oh, indeed, that was interesting. Yes, she could almost certainly be of help.

'He left me three years ago. Without warning, without so much as a pound or two to carry on with.'

Left her suddenly. One morning he went out and didn't come back. And by evening came a telegram saying he wasn't coming back at all – ever. No explanation. No money. Hardly a scrap to eat in the house, and she with a child of two and no job.

Dear, dear; very sorry to hear it.

Maintenance order by the Court?

Oh, yes, certainly – and what was the good of it, seeing he had disappeared?

'I want you to be quite frank with me, madam, and tell me why you changed your name. Are you divorced or living with somebody else, perhaps?'

'Change my name, indeed! I didn't change my name – he did. To avoid me, I've no doubt! But I tracked him down in the end, and now this, just as I was going to get something out of him.'

'Do I understand you to say that Robert Draper was not his real name, but that his name was Robert Wood?'

'Robert George Wood, that's his name. A bad man, who's come to a bad end, as I often told him he would, Inspector.'

Morgan took a foolscap sheet of paper, said:

'Madam, you are certainly being helpful. Would you mind if we take down in writing all you have to tell us?'

Taking a statement is a slow business. So many hesitations and repetitions, so much rambling and irrelevancy, so many questions and answers which then must be reduced to simple clear sentences.

Not long, only an hour or two, but doubtless better than nothing. A girl in her situation needs all the breathing space she can get. One way and another the regulation Metropolitan Police boot is going to crash right down on Gladys, especially as the laboratory have just phoned through to say that the inscription on the watch of Robert Wood, alias Draper, read:

'Robert with love from Gladys.'

*

You couldn't blame the Inspector for the fuss at Gladys Turner's house. It was not his fault at all. The trouble was that bluff Ed Tilling had referred to her in all innocence as Miss Turner. If the Inspector had known she was married he might have arranged things differently; he was a kindly man.

But he didn't know.

So now, as he sat in the small living-room with the upright piano against one wall, and the cheap stores furniture, he tried to think out the best way of putting things in the circumstances.

Out of the corner of his eyes he saw Sergeant Shaw watching him with an expectant look, as though Shaw was confident that he was going to pull off some miracle of tactful manoeuvring.

It had begun on the doorstep, when they had rung the bell, and a man of about thirty-five had opened the door and said briefly:

'Yes?'

'We are police officers,' the Inspector said. 'Is Miss Turner in?'

'Why?'

The instinctive working-class hostility to the police, the defensive attitude, the attempt to gain time even though time could serve no useful purpose.

'I wish to speak to her in connexion with certain inquiries I am making.'

'Why?' said the man again. He was in his shirt sleeves, collarless, a thickset man, with a round bullet-head, hair cut very short, red face, small grey eyes. The eyes suspicious, looking the police officers up and down, the body firmly planted in the doorway with no obvious intention of standing aside to let them in. The feeling that police spelt trouble, unknown trouble, but trouble all the same.

Tension and resentment, and with it the Englishman's determination not to be pushed around, to assert his rights, not to let the police come barging in as though they owned the place.

'I am Chief Detective Inspector Morgan,' began the Inspector, but the man interrupted him.

'There's no Miss Turner lives here.'

'What's your name, who are you?' asked the Sergeant harshly.

'What's that to you? My name's not Miss Turner. Do I look as though my name's Miss Turner?'

'Is there anybody called Turner living at this address?' said the Inspector patiently.

'Yes, there is.'

'Who?'

'Me.'

'Are you her brother?'

'No, I'm not.'

'Is there anybody else called Turner living at this address?'

'There is.'

'Who?'

'My wife. What of it?'

The Inspector hesitated, licked his lips, and said:

'Is your wife's Christian name Gladys, Mr Turner?'

'It is.'

'Then I would like to have a word with her if she is in.'

'Now what is all this, eh? Ringing of bells, and Miss Turner this, and Miss Turner that, and what's your name, and is her name Gladys. What's it all about? That's what I want to know.'

'We are conducting certain investigations –'

'Oh, you are, are you? Well, how do I know you're police officers, that's what I want to know. You might be anybody.'

The last bluster, the last-ditch play for time, the despairing glance at the police car by the kerb with the uniformed driver at the wheel.

'This is my warrant card.'

The man turned slowly, reluctantly, and shouted up the narrow staircase just inside the doorway:

'Gladys! Come down a minute, will you, dear?'

A figure at the top of the stairs said:

'Why? Why, who is it, Len?'

'It's two men who want to speak to you, dear. Police officers, dear. Just come down and see what they want, dear.'

'Bring them into the sitting-room, dear, don't leave them on the doorstep.'

The tone irritable, the police car unseen, the unspoken thought: get them into the house, away from the neighbours' eyes. A pause as she darted into some upstairs room, doubtless to dab powder on her nose. Then footsteps on the stairs, and she came in.

She was about thirty, plump but not fat. Hair naturally blonde, thought the Inspector, but probably artificially curled. China-blue eyes, full lips, nose rather small and shapeless. Doll-like, but a well-rounded, well-fed doll. The type that wouldn't wear.

She came in smoothing out some creases in her blue cotton frock.

'Just been having a bit of shut-eye,' she said, and tried to smile naturally.

The Inspector wished she had not come down in such a hurry, wished she had taken time to put on some lipstick. He took out cigarettes, offered them. She shook her head.

'Not just at the moment, ta.'

The Inspector replaced the cigarettes in his pocket and said:

'I didn't know you were married, Mrs Turner. Mr Tilling referred to you as Miss Turner.'

'Oh, he doesn't know I'm married, either. I knew one of the girls on the staff before I applied for the job, see, and she said he preferred to take on unmarried girls, because married ones sometimes have to stay away for one reason or another, see, or have babies. So I never told him I was married. That's why he called me Miss Turner, see.'

'I see.'

'I suppose you have come about poor Mr Draper?'

'That's right, madam. Just in case you can help us. Mr Tilling didn't really seem to know much about him, but he said you worked in the same room, and perhaps you could tell us something about him.'

'I'll try.'

'How long had you worked in the same room at the office with Mr Draper, madam?'

'About seven months.'

'Did he speak much about himself?'

'Not so much. No, he didn't really. Kind of kept himself to himself.'

The Inspector was watching her feet. They were neatly shod. One leg was crossed over the other. The Inspector

64

always watched people's feet when he was questioning them. He considered them a better indication of tension than hands. A person might consciously control his hands, keep them still. But many people forget about their feet. He watched Gladys Turner's right foot moving slightly up and down, up and down, and said:

'He wasn't the sort of man one got to know easily?'

'Oh, no, he wasn't. He wasn't at all that type.'

'Not a cosy type?'

'Not cosy, no. Kind of distant. You know?'

'Did he have many friends, being that type?'

'He never mentioned any.'

'Any woman friends?'

'Not that I know. I tell you, he didn't talk much about himself.'

There had been the missing doorkey, the missing cash drawings, and there was something missing here, only this time it did not take the Inspector so long to notice it.

There was cooperation in a negative kind of way, mostly agreeing with what he put forward, but no repeated expressions of horror at what had happened, no eager questions. She didn't say, 'Isn't it awful?' or, 'It's horrible, horrible,' or 'I just can't believe it,' or 'He was such a quiet sort of chap, why ever would anybody want to kill Mr Draper?'

She just sat there, foot moving up and down, rather pale, a plump blue-eyed china doll in a blue dress, watching him. Alert and defensive. The Inspector sighed. He wondered what would make her react. The watch with the inscription on the back? Possibly. And possibly not. If she was cute, and for all her china-doll face and plump figure he had an idea she was, then she would point out that Gladys was a very common name.

He couldn't very well say to her, 'Yes, but your name is Gladys, and your foot is moving up and down, showing nervous tension, and your whole attitude indicates perfectly clearly to me that you know a lot about this guy which you are not telling. So come off it, and come clean. What about this watch?'

He couldn't do that. Perhaps some other Gladys had given Draper the watch.

He wished he could get her husband out of the room. He looked at the man. Stolid, beefy, holding a cigarette between the thumb and the first two fingers, lighted end towards the palm of the hand, leaning forward in his chair, elbows on his knees, one hand hanging loose between his legs. Listening intently, aware of his rights as a citizen, eager to assert them, especially if by so doing he could annoy a police officer.

The Inspector stirred irritably, and suddenly said:

'Mrs Turner, had you any reason to believe that Mr Draper was married?'

'Married?'

The foot stopped swaying as Gladys Turner looked at him incredulously.

'Did he ever mention a wife?'

'No, he didn't!' snapped Gladys Turner. 'He always said he couldn't afford to be married, he always said it wasn't fair to marry a girl unless you could keep her nicely; that's what he always said.'

'Well, he was married, all the same, madam.'

'I don't believe it!'

'Why shouldn't he have been?' said Turner suddenly from his corner. 'Why shouldn't the bloke have been married, like the Inspector says? How do you know he wasn't married? He might have been, mightn't he?'

'He lived alone, anyway.'

'How do you know? How do you know he lived alone?' said Turner.

'Because he said he did, that's why,' answered Gladys Turner quickly and sharply.

'He said he did!' mocked Len Turner, and winked heavily at the Inspector, indicating his view that all women were pretty simple, and Gladys among the simplest.

All hostility gone now. The man-to-man wink. Gladys obviously not involved, the police not after her, therefore he could unbend. Basically a friendly chap, Len. Good old Len, to his workmates, and proud of it.

The avalanche was beginning to move now. Up among the mists of the mountain side, where Len couldn't see it, it was beginning to inch its way forward. He couldn't see it, because

66

he wasn't watching Gladys's foot with its nervous movement, and he didn't interpret the meaning of the sharp tone of her replies.

Good old Len.

Honest as they make them, and dumb as an ox. One of the insects. Solid bone from the thorax upwards. And due to be engulfed any moment now, unless a miracle happens.

'Have you any reason to believe that Mr Draper ever used any other name?'

'Any other name?' repeated Gladys, in a surprised tone. 'No, of course he didn't. Why should he?'

'Men have various reasons for changing their names.'

Gladys Turner thought this over for a few seconds.

'Well, he didn't anyway. Bob wasn't a crook.'

'Bob?'

'Mr Draper. We all called him Bob in the office. He wasn't a crook.'

'There could be another reason for changing a name. If a man wished to run away from his wife, for instance.'

'I tell you he wasn't married. Why do you go on and on about his being married?'

The Inspector opened his brief-case, took out a buff-coloured folder.

'Would it surprise you to know that a woman called at Scotland Yard a couple of hours ago and made a statement claiming to be his wife, stating that he ran away from her three years ago and that his real name was Wood?'

Len Turner laughed loudly and slapped his knee in delight.

'There you are, dear, what did I say? Eh? What did I say?'

But nobody paid much attention to Len, who hadn't said anything particularly apposite, anyway.

They let Len get on with it, have his little joke while he could. They were interested in each other, the Inspector and Gladys, and Sergeant Shaw was interested in both for different reasons.

The Inspector watched Gladys Turner, noting the disbelief in her eyes; or if not the disbelief, the reluctance to believe. She said, loudly:

'But is it true, that's what I'd like to know? Maybe she's one of these people who – '

'Who what?' asked the Inspector.

'Who kind of come forward whenever a case gets into the papers. I've read about them. They're barmy, most of them. They just want to attract attention to themselves, that's what they want to do.'

'Perhaps she is that kind of person. I don't know yet. I'm just telling you what she claims. We're checking up among the marriage certificates at Somerset House. We'll soon know if she's telling the truth. I thought I'd just tell you, that's all.'

'Why?' asked Gladys Turner. 'Why should it interest me?'

The Inspector said quickly:

'I don't think you understand, madam. I'm trying to find the person who killed Mr Draper, or Mr Wood, whichever was his name. I've got no leads at all. Time is getting on, and you've got to get cracking in these cases because the longer the time that goes by, the more difficult it is for people to remember important facts. Do you understand me?'

'Of course I understand you.'

The blue eyes wider, the face paler now. The foot still waving up and down, but now the hands at work, too. The forefinger and thumb of the right hand pulling at the forefinger of the left hand. The Inspector said:

'So I'm trying to build up a picture of Mr Draper, as I'll still call him, because maybe I can get an idea of the sort of enemies he had, if any. So that's why I'm putting all these questions, see? I've got to start right at the beginning. I've got nowhere yet. Not even with you.'

'I've told you all I can.'

'Listen,' said the Inspector slowly. 'Listen, and I'll read you a bit of what Mrs Wood said in her statement. "My name is Gertrude Mary Wood, of 324, Angel Way, Ilford. I have been shown the photograph of a person calling himself Robert George Draper, and recognize him as a man I married on May 2nd 1949, who at that time called himself Robert George Wood. The man whom I married in the name of Robert George Wood had recently returned from Germany, where he had been employed in the Accountant-General's Division of

68

the Control Commission (British Element). Shortly after we had gone through a form of marriage ceremony, my husband obtained a post with Messrs Tilling and Ledcot, turf accountants. He was employed by this firm until he left me three years ago. I have not seen him since. I have been shown certain articles which I identify as belonging to him, including a wristwatch, which he stated that he bought with some betting wins. I do not know if the watch had any writing on the back." '

The Inspector paused, looked at Gladys Turner.

'Do you happen to know if the watch had an inscription on the back?'

'How should I know? How should I know if his watch had anything on the back?'

The injured innocence, the plaintive tone, the petulant shrug.

'He might have shown it to you,' suggested Sergeant Shaw loudly. 'Why shouldn't he have shown it to you?'

'Well, he didn't and that's that.'

'But he might have done, mightn't he? Seeing that you knew him so well,' said Shaw.

'I never said I knew him well. What are you trying to get me to say? What's the idea?'

'I'm not trying to get you to say anything,' said Shaw, leaning forward in his chair. 'Except the truth.'

'I'm telling you the truth. Are you calling me a liar?'

Gladys Turner got up out of her chair, began to plump up the cushions angrily, then turned and said:

'Well, if that's all you're wanting, I'll get on with my housework.'

'Who said it is all we're wanting?' said the Inspector mildly.

When she turned and looked at him, he added:

'Can you suggest anybody who might have wished to kill him?'

' 'Course I can't. Otherwise I would have told you.'

'Know anyone who had a grudge against him?' asked Shaw.

'No, I don't.'

'Anyone he might have done a wrong to?' said the Inspector.

'Male or female,' said the Sergeant.

'Either in the past or more recently,' said the Inspector.

'Anybody at all?' asked the Sergeant.

69

'The answer's no, no, no, and no! Now are you satisfied?'

She was standing by the mantelpiece looking down at them seated in their chairs. A big woman, a strong woman, thought the Inspector. Large hips, square shoulders, the arms rounded and well shaped but muscular and the upper arms inclined to thickness.

The Inspector thought: she might have done it, she's strong enough. She could have heaved him into the open divan, a little at a time. And then gone out and got some petrol from somewhere. But would she have had the nerve, the foolishness, to walk through the streets with a can of petrol? No, she wouldn't.

He said:

'How do you think Mr Draper managed to keep that flat up on the comparatively small salary he earned at your firm?'

'He won money on horses, he said. He had a system.'

'Did he tell it to you?'

She shook her head, tapping with her foot on the ground, anxious for them to be gone.

'You agree that on his salary alone he would have found it difficult to keep up that flat?'

She replied sullenly, reluctantly:

'He might have done. So what?'

'So nothing,' said Shaw. 'We just want to know, that's all.'

'He might have done.'

'How do you know?' asked Shaw in his hard voice. 'How do you know what the flat is like?' he added quickly, head thrust forward. 'You said he kept himself to himself, you said you didn't know much about him.'

'You implied he was just an office acquaintance,' pointed out the Inspector.

'So how do you know what the flat was like, eh?'

Shaw again. Thrusting, eager. And quite ruthless.

'Tell us that. Come on, we're waiting; we haven't got all day. We're busy.'

Len stirred, straightened his position, said:

'Here, don't you bully her.'

'Who's bullying her?'

Shaw swung round to glare at him.

'She don't need to answer nothing, if she don't want to,' said Len, his eyes on Gladys.

Uneasiness in the voice now. The feeling that all was not as it should be, that something was wrong somewhere, but the inability to diagnose where. Even Len can hear the first sounds of the avalanche now, only he doesn't know it's an avalanche, and he doesn't know the size of it. All he can hear is something stirring somewhere.

Still it's better than nothing. Good old Len.

'He described it to me,' said Gladys Turner, turning her back on the room to look for something on the mantelpiece. 'He often said how nice it was.'

'But you never went there?' asked Shaw.

' 'Course I never went there. Why should I?'

'I'm not asking you why you should have done, I'm asking you whether you had been there.'

'No, I haven't, and what's more I don't like the tone of your questions. Len, I'm fed up with this, proper fed up. Have I got to go on answering all these questions? I haven't, have I?'

'You've got to help the police if you can,' said Len surprisingly.

He was looking at her now, thoughtfully, eyes dull and unblinking as though something was moving in the sluggish stuff in his head. Beginning to move quite quickly, too, like the thing in the mists of the mountainside above him.

Gladys Turner went quickly to the door, and said:

'I could do with a cup of tea.'

She went out. They could hear her running the water-tap, filling the kettle. Then the plop as she lit the gas stove. Nobody said anything. They all watched her as she came back slowly into the room, and began fiddling with her cigarette.

'Why do you do that?' asked the Inspector bleakly.

'Do what?'

'Why do you prick it with a pin, near the end?'

'It burns longer that way,' said Len. 'Somebody told her about it. It cools the smoke, too. Where's your holder?' he added.

'Upstairs.'

'I've never seen anybody prick a cigarette like that before,'

71

said Sergeant Shaw with exaggerated casualness. He looked at the Inspector. 'I should think that's a very rare habit, wouldn't you, sir? Making a hole in a cigarette about an inch from the end. Very uncommon, that.'

The Inspector nodded, thinking quickly, trying to fathom some way of getting Gladys Turner by herself. He was quite prepared to break Gladys or Len, or both, to smash the marriage if need be, because murder is murder, and the police machine cannot be halted for the Gladyses and Lens of this world.

But he was willing and eager to avoid causing trouble if he could. He said politely:

'Mrs Turner, I expect there are a lot of minor points you could clear up, and then perhaps we could put them on paper. I've got a nice car outside. What about popping down to the local police station with me?'

He spoke softly, persuasively, looking her in the eyes, seriously and earnestly. She was no fool. Something in his manner told her that what he was proposing was in her own interests.

He saw the hesitation in her eyes.

Len Turner said:

'Why? Why should she go to the station?'

'I thought she might like to, that's all,' said the Inspector slowly.

'Get rid of us, so to speak,' said Shaw. 'Get us out of the way of the neighbours. Prevent too much gossip.'

'She needn't come in the car, if she doesn't want to,' said Morgan. 'Might look bad. She can come on her own. It's only five minutes' walk.'

'Well, she's not going. She can say anything she's got to say here, and I've plenty of paper if you want to write stuff down.'

Len looked at her, seeking approval for his stand.

But she said:

'I don't mind going down to the station. I'll walk down.'

'I'll go with you,' said Len stoutly. 'You don't want to go down there on your own. You might get in a muddle.'

' 'Course I won't get in a muddle,' said Gladys irritably.

'Anyway, why can't he ask his questions here?' said Len,

doubling on his tracks. 'What's wrong with here? That's what I want to know.'

'Oh, why can't you keep out of it?' snapped Gladys.

He looked at her, hurt by her attitude. Sensing quite clearly now that something was wrong somewhere, but determined stubbornly to keep on his course. There was something a bit fishy going on, and he wasn't going to stand for it. No, he wasn't. He was master in his own house, and always had been and always would be, and Gladys was his wife, and if Gladys had been up to any bloody nonsense, well, let her come out with it.

Good old Len.

The type that won't be saved, a delight to any spirit with a sense of humour. Len in his shirt sleeves, collarless and tieless, stocky and bullet-headed, and red in the face now, listening to the roar of the approaching avalanche, and guessing what it is and not caring. Just standing there in its path shaking his fist at it obstinately.

So now he said doggedly:

'If you gentlemen have any questions to ask my wife, you can ask them in my presence, and that's flat.'

'Perhaps she would rather talk to us alone,' said the Inspector despairingly.

'Yes, I would,' said Gladys Turner defiantly.

'Me and my wife have no secrets from each other,' persisted Len, ignoring her.

'Oh, for God's sake shut your trap, you put me off,' shouted Gladys. 'You do really, sitting there looking at me and interrupting all the time.'

She flung the remains of her cigarette into the empty fireplace.

'I'm going down to the police station, Len, and that's flat. You stay here. You can start peeling the potatoes.'

Len Turner got heavily out of his chair, and went and stood in front of the door. The Inspector and the Sergeant got up out of their chairs, and collected their belongings, and began to move towards the door. Gladys Turner made to go with them.

The Inspector said:

'Perhaps you would stand aside, Mr Turner.'

Len Turner said, not moving:

'She's not leaving this house.'

'Stand aside, there's a good chap,' said the Inspector gently. 'You don't want to be charged with obstructing the police in the course of their duties, do you? That wouldn't do you any good at all, would it? That would be silly, wouldn't it?'

Len Turner did not look at his wife as he spoke. He addressed her through the Inspector. He said:

'You can tell her, if she leaves this house now she can bloody well stay out, that's what. She can take her bloody clothes with her, too, because the door will be bloody well locked when she comes back.'

'All right,' said Gladys bitterly. 'All right, I'll stay here.'

Len Turner relaxed.

'Now then,' he said, 'go ahead.'

The Inspector sat down again. There was nothing more he could do to save them. He couldn't afford to waste any more time. He said:

'I should like you to give me an account of your movements on the night Mr Draper was killed, Mrs Turner. I have reason to believe that you were in Mr Draper's flat on the night that he was murdered. Is that correct?'

'Yes, it was.'

'Would it not have been more frank to tell us that at once?'

'How could I?' replied Gladys Turner. 'How could I? With him there glowering at me, putting me off? How could I tell you?'

'Why did you go to Mr Draper's flat?'

' 'Cause he asked me to.'

'Had you been there before?'

'Yes.'

'How many times?'

'Quite a few.'

'When did you first go there?'

'About six months ago.'

The Inspector hesitated. Finally he said:

'Were you fond of each other, so to speak?'

74

'He said he was fond of me. Otherwise I wouldn't have gone with him. I used to be fond of him. I hate him now, even though he is dead. But I didn't kill him, and you can put that down in your notebooks, see?'

She looked across at her husband and repeated it, her voice shaking:

'I hate him, but I didn't kill him.'

But Len wasn't looking at her. He wasn't looking at the Inspector or the Sergeant either. As far as anybody could tell, Len might not have heard her speak. He was staring out of the window into the hot dusty street, and except that he sometimes passed his tongue over his lips, he was sitting quite still.

The Inspector said:

'Well, we all make mistakes now and then, Mrs Turner.'

'He's only himself to blame,' said Gladys defensively, still looking at her husband. 'I warned him, time and again, I did. You can't say I didn't warn you, Len. I said to him, "It's all very well for you, Len," I said, "with your darts club, and your dog-racing, and your football on Saturday afternoons, and your fishing, and your this and that; but what about me? What about me, sitting here at home," I said. "I do a job, same as you," I said. "I spend my lunch hour rushing about buying things for supper, and then rushing back to do the housework, and cook and wash and iron, and what do I get out of it?" I am just an unpaid housekeeper, that's all I am. And he knows it,' added Gladys Turner, nodding her head at her husband.

As an attempt to turn the tables, to shed the mantle of guilt and don the coat of injured innocence, the Inspector thought it quite a good effort. Not that it would work, of course.

When stocky, bullet-headed men like Len Turner fasten on to an idea, it takes more than a flow of eloquence, a spate of feminine accusations, to shake them.

Len Turner stopped looking out into the street. He had been filling in his football pools coupons, and the coupons and a pen and a pencil lay on a little table by his chair. He looked down at them now, and picked up the pencil, and began to twiddle it, and turn it over and over with his fingers.

'What made you hate him?' asked Len slowly, and thereby

saved the Inspector the necessity of asking the same question. He spoke without looking up. It was only when she did not reply that he raised his eyes and stared at her.

'Go on, you slut, don't sit there like a stuffed owl – what made you hate him?'

She began to cry, sniffing and dabbing at her eyes. After a few seconds he answered for her.

'There's only one bloody thing makes a slut like you hate a man. He let you down, didn't he? Eh? He promised you the earth, and when the pinch came, he let you down, eh? Wouldn't stand by you, would he? He got what he wanted and – '

The blood rushing to the head, the voice choking at the thought. The pencil snapped between the strong fingers, and thrown across the room into the empty grate.

Len was on his feet now, very red in the face, sweat on his forehead, his fists clenched. Self-control vanishing as the enormity of the thing began to sweep over him in waves, as his imagination got to work.

First the stunned surprise, then the hot, raging indignation, that's the way it always went, thought the Inspector, and said softly, persuasively:

'Take it easy, Mr Turner; she's not the first to have a slip up, and not the last. These things happen in the best-regulated families, as it were.'

But Len wasn't having any of that stuff, any more than he was shaken by Gladys's counter-attack. He took a step towards her, and when the Inspector put out a restraining arm, he leaned forward and shouted:

'He wouldn't stand by you, would he? You're in the family way, aren't you, you dirty rotten little bitch?'

'No, I'm not!'

'Go on, admit it!'

'No!'

He watched her sobbing for a few seconds, then shouted again:

'Then what are you so bloody upset about, eh? Tell me that? And don't give me any of that slop stuff about loving me really, 'cos a bitch like you doesn't know the truth from bloody lies. You're going to have his kid, aren't you? That's what you're going to do, have his bloody kid.'

He paused, and wiped the sweat from his brow with his forearm, then shouted:

'I left the Navy for you, you bitch, just to please you. Left the Navy to marry a whore and bring up a bastard brat, like what you're going to have. Go on, admit it,' he went on, back again on the theme, 'don't sit there snivelling. You're in the family way aren't you? Eh?'

She might have accepted it if the police officers had not been there; the insults and the jeers and the reproaches, even a beating up. She might have taken it all, and still kept silent about certain things.

But it was different in front of strangers. She couldn't listen to the insults and the coarse names in front of others. The sobs ceased, and the blood rushed to her face as it had to Len's.

'All right,' she said angrily. 'All right then, you asked for it, and you can have it, and serve you damn well right, Len Turner. I am –'

Her voice died away. But she had no need to finish the sentence. She could tell that by looking at Len's face.

Maybe he had hoped for the best all the time, had been pressing her in the hope that she would go on denying it, that in the end he would believe her; that even if he never wholly and entirely believed her, at least he could have some hope in his heart that he was wrong.

But Gladys Turner didn't see that, of course, and Len didn't see the danger of pressing her too far in front of others.

So Len, unexpectedly, turned very white, because there was no more hope left. He was still white in the face as he swung round and picked up his jacket and stumbled to the door and into the little hall and out of the house.

Gladys shouted his name twice, once when he was lurching towards the living-room door, and once when she heard the front door slam.

But he took no notice. None of the Good Old Lens ever do.

Out in the kitchen the kettle had begun to boil, and the steam was forcing its way through a patent device on the spout, filling the house with a shrill, high-pitched scream.

It was like a fiendish boatswain's pipe whistling Len out of his own home into some dense mental jungle of his own creation, where garish birds stretched their necks to mock him as he went stumbling by.

Chapter 5

THERE comes a time in a successful murder investigation when quite suddenly the case begins to crack open, when people begin to remember small things which they realize may be of help to the police, when others, who may have held back from reasons of fear or self-interest, overcome their reluctance to come forward and to say what they know.

Chief Detective Inspector Morgan thought that such a moment had arrived when he came back to the Yard after his interview with Gladys Turner and found James Bleaker waiting to see him.

He had the lawyer sent up to his room at once, and when Bleaker came in he rose to meet him, and greeted him cordially, motioning him to be seated and offering him a cigarette.

Shaw, by his brusque, openly suspicious manner, put people on their guard. Morgan, by his manner, invited confidences. Although he could be as tough as Shaw when the occasion demanded it, at other times Morgan was the benevolent uncle, the soothing and sympathetic listener. More than one murderer had fallen into the Morgan trap.

So now Morgan said:

'Well, now, Mr Bleaker, what can we do to help you?'

Bleaker did not reply at once. He sat in the uncomfortable upright visitor's chair, with his bony red hands and wrists protruding as usual from the sleeves of his black jacket, and stared at the Inspector with his watery blue eyes. He was wearing a none too clean white collar of the old-fashioned butterfly type, a grey tie with an imitation pearl tie-pin, and the inevitable striped trousers. His black shoes had the cracked faded look of cheap footwear which is old and is not regularly cleaned.

Like his hands, his face was red and bony, his hair thin, grey, and untidy. He brought into the room with him a smell of spirits.

Gazing at Bleaker, waiting for him to reply, watching him lick his loose, moist lips, the Inspector could not imagine why any woman should accept James Bleaker as a lover, but then the Inspector had thought the same thing about many men in his time.

'Well?' said the Inspector after some seconds.

Bleaker licked his lips again. Then, abruptly, in his high-pitched voice, he said:

'You can call off your men from following me.'

'My men are not following you.'

The Inspector pressed a button on his desk, and added: 'Why should anybody be following you, sir?'

Bleaker said:

'I didn't expect you to admit it, but I saw them. Last night and this morning, and I don't like it. If I have any more of it, I shall put in a complaint to the Commissioner of Police in person.'

Morgan said nothing, waiting for Shaw, and when the Sergeant put his head round the door, the Inspector said:

'Come in, Sergeant. Mr Bleaker, here, says that we have some men following him about. I take it he is imagining things.'

'He is, sir,' said Shaw tonelessly, and walked across to the window and stood leaning against the sill, glaring at Bleaker.

'There's a lot of people think they're being followed by the police, sir.'

'I often wonder why,' said the Inspector mildly.

'So do I, sir. In many cases, I expect it's vanity or conceit.'

Bleaker swung round on his chair, passed the back of his hand across his wet lips, and said:

'Are you being insulting? Are you getting at me?'

The Inspector saw Shaw's lower lip come forward, and imagined the ginger hackles rising on the back of the Sergeant's neck.

'I said "in many cases", sir, not in all cases. I should have thought you would have heard me say that, sir. I'm not aware that I mumble, sir.'

The Inspector said quickly:

'Nobody is following you, Mr Bleaker. And nobody is insulting you, either. Now is there anything else?'

Bleaker hesitated, stubbed out his half-smoked cigarette in an ash-tray on the Inspector's desk, pulled out a packet from his pocket, and lit another cigarette.

'Yes, there is; it's about Draper.'

'What about Draper?' asked Shaw, still ruffled.

Bleaker ignored Shaw and spoke directly to the Inspector:

'I am prepared to give you certain information which may be of assistance to you in your investigations – upon certain conditions.'

The Inspector looked at Bleaker and then said:

'Am I to understand that unless certain conditions are fulfilled you propose deliberately to withhold information from the police, sir?'

'In a murder case, too,' added Sergeant Shaw.

'Yes,' said Bleaker, 'that's just what you are to understand.'

'I suppose you are aware of what you are saying, sir,' said the Inspector politely, 'and in front of a witness.'

'I don't want money.'

The Inspector shook his head firmly.

'I'm not accepting information with conditions attached to it. The cock won't fight, Mr Bleaker.'

'The conditions are simple – that you don't call upon me as a material witness, and that you treat my information as strictly confidential.'

'Look, Mr Bleaker, how can I guarantee whether the Director of Public Prosecutions will, or will not, call upon you to give evidence? How can I pledge the word of the D.P.P.? As to treating the information as confidential, I will do all I can to cover the source of the information. I can't say more than that.'

The Inspector looked out of the window, purposely casual, to give Bleaker more time to think before answering.

The storm-clouds were gathering again. For a second or two he thought of Len Turner wandering somewhere in London with a heart full of pain.

Then he heard Bleaker stir uneasily on his hard chair, and

turned his gaze back from the window, back to Bleaker's bony face and uneasy light blue eyes.

'All right,' said Bleaker, 'here's one thing. Draper's real name was Wood.'

'I know that,' said the Inspector. 'I know all about that, sir. Also the fact that he was married.'

'You know where he worked, of course?'

'Yes, sir.'

'Did you know he had a sideline? Did you know that? Quite a lucrative one, which enabled him to live as he did?'

'I believe he betted quite heavily, sir.'

'This wasn't a gamble, this was a certainty.'

'I'd be glad to know what that was,' said the Inspector eagerly. 'Yes, sir, that would be helpful; I'd like to know that.'

'I expect you would,' said Bleaker, and paused, and looked at the glowing end of his cigarette.

'It was blackmail,' he added with a kind of studied nonchalance. 'Blackmail, that's what it was.'

He glanced up quickly to see the effect of his words, and then down again at his cigarette end.

Outside on the Embankment the traffic droned along by the side of the Thames. From nearby Big Ben above the Houses of Parliament came the measured chimes of the hour. Almost automatically the Inspector glanced at his watch. Six o'clock. Out of the corner of his eye he saw Shaw watching him, waiting for a lead.

'Is that so?' said the Inspector at last. 'And whom was he blackmailing, can you tell us that, sir?'

'I can.'

Bleaker hesitated, gazing past Shaw through the open window, watching the massing clouds. The storm looming up again. A distant flash of sheet lightning flickered on the horizon, and some seconds later came a faint and muffled grumble of thunder. The Inspector watched the smoke curling up from Bleaker's cigarette, winding its way over his yellow-stained fingers, dispersing as it climbed up his dingy black jacket.

James Bleaker, the lawyer, sat very still. Chief Detective Inspector Morgan, the Celt, guessed intuitively at the struggle going on in his mind, and gave Shaw a warning look. He didn't want Shaw flinging some quick, harsh question at a man in Bleaker's state. He felt the tension rising in Bleaker's mind.

Outside in the corridor came the sound of footsteps and voices. The footsteps stopped outside the room. The Inspector recognized the deep voice of an Inspector in the fraud squad, and held his breath in case the man might wish to consult him, afraid that he might knock on the door, afraid of any disturbance. The Inspector looked at Bleaker's pale-blue eyes and watched them flicker nervously towards him, and then towards the door. It was as if he were watching the needle of a delicate precision instrument which the slightest disturbance might wreck.

He knew now why Bleaker had brought a smell of whisky into the room with him. Bleaker had been bolstering up his courage, or quieting his conscience. Perhaps both.

The Inspector saw the Adam's apple in Bleaker's throat move up and down once or twice behind the butterfly wings of his collar, and at the same time the voices in the corridor moved on, and became fainter. Bleaker said:

'Otto Steiner, that's whom he was blackmailing.'

'I see. Are you sure?'

'Would I say it, if I wasn't sure?'

'You realize the implications of what you are saying?'

Bleaker nodded, and passed his tongue over his lips, and remained silent.

'You are supposed to be his legal adviser, you know.'

Again Bleaker nodded without speaking.

'You realize that what you have said provides a motive for the murder of this man Draper?'

'Of course I realize it,' snapped Bleaker in his high-pitched voice.

'Why didn't you tell us this before?' asked Shaw in his hard tones. 'Why have you been keeping all this to yourself, sir?'

The Inspector said smoothly:

'Never mind that now, sir. Let's get back to the point. How was this chap Draper blackmailing Steiner? That's the important thing. And how do you come to know about it?'

'This is how it is,' said Bleaker earnestly. 'I've got a lady friend called Renate Brueckmann. We're going to get married one day. She's my fiancée, really. She's been staying with me. You know that, of course. But before that, she was sort of engaged to this man Draper. Well she used to live in the same district in Hamburg as the Steiners. In fact, the two families knew each other quite well. Both of them were anti-Hitler, see, but Otto and Rose Steiner and Renate Brueckmann, they weren't Communists. Liberals, a bit radical you might say, but not Communists, not Reds, see?'

James Bleaker stopped and looked down at his cigarette.

'Weren't Communists?' repeated the Inspector. 'What's that got to do with it?'

'What's Communism got to do with blackmail?' asked Shaw. 'Being a Communist isn't a crime. You can't blackmail a man for that. Anyway, you said Steiner wasn't a Communist.'

'He wasn't,' said Bleaker. 'But –'

The Inspector was staring at Bleaker, watching the Adam's apple go up and down again, watching the left hand pick at a loose thread in the knee of the well-worn striped trousers.

'Go on,' said the Inspector, and noted how the feeling of depression was spreading from the nerves in his stomach, reaching throughout his body in waves.

He felt suddenly tired. What had started as an intriguing if infuriating investigation was becoming meshed about in tragedy, bearing the aspects of a case where the victim deserved what he got, and that was the type of case he hated.

'Go on,' said the Inspector again, and saw the puzzled look on Shaw's face. He was a long jump ahead of Shaw. Shaw was an excellent assistant, dealing punctiliously and swiftly with events as they occurred. A typical Anglo-Saxon, swift to improvise, practical, but reluctant or unable to look ahead, to allow the mind to range around. Shaw couldn't see what was coming now.

'You've got to get the picture of things as they were under Hitler,' said Bleaker, and when the Sergeant stirred irritably the Inspector shot him a warning look.

Bleaker was beating up to his point gradually, tacking against

83

the winds of his conscience. Better to be patient. Let him do it his own way. Get a clearer picture in the end. Better to be understanding, to take time, rather than to hustle him, to make him sullen and taciturn.

'Go on,' said the Inspector for the third time.

Bleaker swallowed and said:

'It was like this. After the other Parties, the Social Democrats and the rest, had all begun to pack up under Hitler, the German Communist Party seemed to many people to be the only one left which might have some hope of resisting him. So a lot of people joined it, see? Even though they weren't Communists, see? And when the Party had to go underground, and work in secret, it was even more attractive to some of the younger, adventurous Germans.'

'Such as?' asked the Inspector, and waited for the answer he knew was coming, and which, when it was spoken, sent his mind ranging in search of the question which so often worried him: what was Justice? Which was the greater crime, blackmail and the torture and murder of the soul, or the sudden blow and murder of the body?

'Such as Julius Steiner,' muttered James Bleaker, 'now in America and holding down a good job – so far.'

'What sort of job?'

'In a big engineering firm carrying out important United States government contracts. Of course, you've got to have rules,' added Bleaker hastily. 'I'm not criticizing. You can't see into every man's mind, can you? Anybody could say he joined the Party though he wasn't a Marxist at heart, and you can't tell whether he is telling the truth or not, can you? So you've got to have a rule, I know that. Security is Security. And you've got to have rules, haven't you?

'The innocent may be compelled to suffer with the guilty for the sake of the community, that's what I say. It's too bad, but it can't be helped, that's what I always say. You've got to have rules. Only this Julius Steiner kid, he wasn't a Communist when he joined the Party, and never has been.'

'That's as may be,' said the Inspector slowly, 'but how do you know?'

'Well, that's what Renate Brueckmann says, and she knew

him like a sister. She knew the whole family. He talked to her quite frankly. She's certain he wasn't a real Communist. And his parents, they are sure he wasn't either. Just anti-Hitler, see?'

'And his parents, and none of the Steiner family or the Brueckmann family were Communists or Communist sympathizers?'

'That's right. They were violently anti-Hitler and violently anti-Communist. Especially Otto Steiner.'

'Maybe Julius Steiner hid his true political feelings because he didn't want to distress them?'

James Bleaker shrugged despairingly.

'Maybe, but it doesn't make any difference to this case, does it?'

'No,' conceded the Inspector, and sighed. 'No, it doesn't make any difference, really.'

He began to fiddle with the paper-knife on his desk.

'I suppose your German lady friend told Draper?'

Breaker nodded.

'Just casually, one evening. He got to know her in Germany when he was there with the Control Commission, and she looked him up when she came to England, and they – well, they got more friendly. And she happened to mention the fact to him as a matter of interest. It was after that that he began to have more money to spend. He said it was from backing horses.'

'And she believed him?'

'At first. Then she kind of stopped thinking about his source of income. Sort of took things for granted.'

'How long did the blackmailing go on?'

'A couple of years.'

'How much was Draper getting off Steiner?'

'I don't know. Neither does Renate. But it must have been a fair amount. Several hundred a year, to judge by the way he lived.'

'All just to make him keep his mouth shut about Julius Steiner having been in the Communist Party?'

'He's worked his way up in the firm, see? Got a good position now. Wife and children, too. You know how attached

Jews are to their families. The old man figured he'd rather pay up than see his son's career wrecked.'

The Inspector nodded.

The insults and the humiliation, the near-ruin, the flight to England, and a new life. The children doing well, thank you, especially Julius, the only son.

Julius getting his first promotion. Rising steadily in the firm. The marriage and the grandchildren. More promotion and a fine career ahead. Then the knife-thrust from the blue.

Pay up, or take the consequences.

Behind the drone of the traffic along the Embankment the Inspector heard Steiner's words: 'God has been merciful to us so far.' The perfect humility, the unselfish gratitude. The children were alive and doing well – so far.

You worked and scraped and saved to pay the bloodsucker Draper, but that didn't matter so very much, because you had always worked hard and demanded little, except for the children. Your tastes were simple, your interests centred in the family. All was going well.

Then business wasn't so good.

You found it hard to pay, and tried to soften the heart of your torturer, and when he only laughed and pointed out that you could sell up your shop and home, what then?

What happened then?

The Inspector had a mental picture of Steiner, the Jew, driven to despair, the heart that had borne so much now nearly broken; the balance of the mind disturbed, the red mist, the decision to end it all, to make sure that even if all else was lost, the mouth of Robert George Draper should be closed for ever.

Thus ran the imagination of Chief Detective Inspector Morgan. Aloud he said:

'And what then?'

'What then?'

'How did she find out that Drapr ewas using the information she had given him?'

'He told her, that's how she found out. If he hadn't told her, she would probably never have known. They had a row, because she found out he was carrying on with other women and she told him she was going to leave him.

86

'Then he said, "Well, you needn't think I'm the sort of guy you can leave flat, because I'm not, see?" He said he could make things difficult for her, as she was an alien, and when that didn't work, he said, "Well, I've got your friends the Steiners where I want 'em, thanks to Julius having been in the Communist Party, and if you try and leave me flat, I'll make it even hotter for them." That's what he said, or words to that effect.'

'And then?'

'She wasn't falling for that one, either. She just packed her bags and cleared out, but she was a bit uneasy, and went straight round to Otto Steiner and asked him what it was all about. He told her.'

The Inspector opened a drawer in his desk, and took out a sheet of foolscap paper.

'I take it you have no objection to making a formal statement incorporating what you have just told us, Mr Bleaker?'

'I have.'

'May I ask why, sir?'

'I told you at the beginning that this information was confidential, didn't I?'

Sergeant Shaw looked at Morgan and said sharply:

'We'll have a word with Miss Brueckmann. Maybe she won't be so finicky as Mr Bleaker, sir.'

Bleaker turned his head and said:

'Miss Brueckmann left for Germany this morning, Sergeant. On holiday, see?'

'Then we'll have her brought back,' snapped Shaw. 'Brought back and questioned.'

Bleaker said sarcastically:

'Doubtless she has committed some crime justifying extradition? I suppose you've got enough evidence to support an application for extradition? I suppose there's an extradition treaty between this country and the West German Government, is there? I suppose you know whether there is or not, do you?'

'Look, sir,' said Morgan, 'will you tell us what made you come forward today and volunteer information which you have been keeping to yourself? I'd be grateful if you'd tell us that.'

Bleaker nodded.

'I thought you'd ask that.'

He extracted another cigarette from his packet, brought out a cheap metal lighter and applied the flame. Morgan thought: the hand steady, but the foot moving slowly up and down. The nervousness consciously controlled in the hands, but the feet forgotten, always the feet forgotten.

'Well?' asked Morgan quietly.

Bleaker took a deep breath and said:

'Yes, I'll tell you that. I was going to tell you that, anyway. It's what I came here for, really. Renate and I, we were at Draper's flat the evening he was killed. For all I know, we were the last people to see him alive – except for the chap who killed him. That's why I came to tell you the story. That's the reason.'

He looked from one to the other of the police officers, as if seeking some sign of astonishment, or some encouragement to continue.

'And why did you call there, sir?' asked Morgan evenly.

'She asked me to come with her.'

'Miss Brueckmann?'

Bleaker nodded.

'It was a kind of bluff, in a way. She was horrified by what had been happening, and she persuaded me to come along and see Draper, and tell him that if he didn't lay off blackmailing Steiner – and if he didn't start paying back the money he had had – she was going to the police, whether the Steiners liked it or not, and that in blackmail cases in this country the police will usually agree to withhold the names of prosecutors and even some of the witnesses.'

'How did he react to that?'

'He just laughed,' replied Bleaker lamely, 'that's all. He just laughed, and said, go ahead. So it didn't work. Not that it matters now, of course.'

'I see, sir.'

Morgan thought for a few seconds.

'You won't mind me pointing out that you have only partly answered my question, sir – about why you withheld the information in the first place, and why you have now come forward.'

88

'Does it matter?'

'It might, sir.'

'It's something you wouldn't understand.' Bleaker spoke with an unexpected note of bitterness in his voice. 'You and the Sergeant, with your set careers and regular money and pensions and things.'

'I don't quite follow, sir.'

'Don't quite follow! Of course you don't quite follow! I never thought you would follow. You don't know what it is to be one of a large working-class family, and educate yourself with State aid, and scrape and save and study half the night to pass your law exams. And then what?'

James Bleaker, solicitor, raised his hands in a curiously pathetic gesture.

'And then what?' he said again, but in a louder, almost strident voice. 'Then you're like me, and thousands of others, spending your life scratching around to make ends meet. Defending the odd petty crook, dealing with cheap landlord-and-tenant squabbles, separation orders, paternity orders. Cheap muck like that, with an occasional juicy house-con-veyancing job to show you what you've missed.

'Well, I'm sorry for Otto Steiner, but I've got my business going better these days, and I'm not sticking my neck out for him or anybody else, and that's flat.'

'There's also the question of justice, sir.'

As soon as he had said it, Morgan realized how smug it sounded, and that it would have the opposite effect to that which he had had in mind.

'I'm not interested in justice,' retorted Bleaker violently. 'I'm interested in me, that's all. I started out with some idea of serving the community and bunk like that, and now the community can get on with it as far as I am concerned. And so can Steiner. As soon as you started having me followed – and you needn't bother to deny it again – I knew I'd end up by coming here. A nice bit of good it would do my practice to get mixed up on the wrong side of the police in a case like this, wouldn't it? That's why I'm here. Steiner or no Steiner, client or no client, I'm keeping my nose clean, and I don't care who suffers, so long as it's not me.'

He was sitting on the edge of his chair now, leaning forward, supporting himself with his hands on his knees. His iron-grey hair was ruffled, his face very red, the moist lips hanging looser than ever, because self-control had been drowned by indignation and self-pity.

Morgan thought he looked like a lean and tousled mongrel dog which had had the worst of it in a fight. He contented himself with saying:

'Well, whatever the reason, Mr Bleaker, I'm sure you've acted correctly in coming forward.'

When Bleaker had relaxed and begun to fumble for the inevitable cigarette, he added:

'You'll understand that as a result of what you've said, I must ask you certain obvious questions?'

'Time of arrival, time of departure, that sort of stuff?'

'That's correct.'

'All right. Miss Brueckmann and I arrived at about seven-forty-five in the evening, and left again at about eight-fifteen.'

'Did you see anybody else on your way in or on your way out?'

'Nobody.'

'Did Draper say he was expecting anybody?'

'No.'

'Did you notice whether Mr Steiner was still in the shop?'

'I don't know whether he was there or not. You couldn't tell. The evening being light, he wouldn't have had to switch the electricity on.' Bleaker shook his head. 'No, I couldn't say one way or the other.'

'Did anybody see you and Miss Brueckmann leave, sir?'

'You mean can anybody confirm the time we left?'

'If you like to put it that way, sir. Just a routine question, of course.'

'Well, nobody saw us leave, as far as I know.'

'May I ask how you got in, sir?'

Bleaker hesitated, then blurted out the answer, jealousy and resentment in his voice.

'Renate, she still had her key. The one Draper had given her.'

'Did Steiner receive three keys from you, when he bought the lease?'

90

'That's right, three.' Bleaker paused. 'Why he told you he only received two, I don't know, but he is like that – he'll make sudden, panicky, untrue answers, because he's so nervy. Poor bloke.'

'Does Miss Brueckmann know you intended to call here and give information?'

Bleaker licked his lips and blinked his watery eyes.

'No, she doesn't know. She wouldn't understand either. She would think I ought to stick my neck out on account of Otto Steiner. She's very fond of them. I'd be very grateful if you could try and not let her know, Inspector.'

Bleaker hesitated, then added:

'She's a wonderful woman. German, of course, but a wonderful woman. I've knocked around with a lot of bints in my time, of course, but she's – '

He paused, searching for the right words.

'She's the only one I've ever really fallen for, and I can't see what she sees in me. She came to see me about Draper, after she had seen the Steiners, and we fell for each other almost at once. Amazing, really. She's already started cleaning me up. Made me order a new suit, and so on. Women are funny, aren't they?'

He looked almost youthful and boyish as he spoke.

'Can't see what she sees in me,' he muttered again, picking at the loose thread in his trousers.

But I can, thought Inspector Morgan. She's fallen for you because you're such a ruddy awful mess, physically and psychologically, that you're a challenge to her maternal instincts, her ingenuity, and her will-power – you're going to be sorted out, and heaven help you, James Bleaker.

Chapter 6

WHAT about good old Len, what's he up to all this time? Any Minister of State, clergyman, or old lady, with a taste for crime would doubtless have enjoyed watching good old Len as he stumbled out of his council house, because that is the sort of thing which happens in murder investigations.

Len was a by-product of the Paton Street case by this time, but a very minor one. He wasn't the victim, and he wasn't the murderer, and he wasn't even a vital witness, so he was of no importance to the police or the general public.

But he was of considerable importance to himself. In fact, he was just as important to himself as Napoleon was to Napoleon, or Alexander the Great was to Alexander the Great.

It was silly of Len the By-Product not to see himself in his true light, and very foolish of him to keep harping in his mind on what might have been, as he took an Underground ticket to Piccadilly Circus, but that's the way he was made.

The only reason why he took a ticket to Piccadilly Circus was because he was tired of tramping around his own neighbourhood and meeting people in the streets whom he knew, and who gave him odd glances as he strode by without so much as a word of greeting for them.

Piccadilly Circus was a long way away, which served his purpose, but it was very hot indeed in the carriages. He sat swaying to the movements of the train, and perspiring, and thinking about Gladys and the pain in his stomach which ebbed and flowed with his thoughts.

Sometimes it was dull and heavy, like a lump of over-warm lead, and sometimes it shot through him like a red-hot knife, making him want to get up, and walk up and down the train; but he couldn't do that, so he just sat and sweated, and let the moisture run down from his forehead into his eyes without even bothering to wipe it away.

Foreigners think that the English are a phlegmatic race, but such is not the case. They are not stolid, because they have such mixed blood. There was a time, in the eighteenth century, when it is said that it was the fashion for the upper classes to ape the imperturbability of the stoic Romans, but Len was not a member of the upper classes, nor was he living in the eighteenth century.

There wasn't much *sang-froid anglais* about Len, as he shoved his way along the crowded pavement in Piccadilly to Hyde Park.

Then, suddenly, almost before he was aware of it, there he was by the lake, lying face down under some trees, his barrel-like chest pressing into the dry earth, and his hands clutching at the sward.

People were rowing boats on the lake, and by the water's edge were some children, and two dogs barking excitedly, and across the water other people were bathing in the Lido.

But Len, he couldn't hear the sound of oars in rowlocks, or children's voices, or the distant laughter and shouts from the Lido. He couldn't even hear the dogs barking. All he could hear was Gladys's voice, all snarly and bitter, saying:

'All right, then, you asked for it, and you can have it, and serve you damn well right, Len Turner. I am –'

Sometimes he groaned a little. Sometimes he just screwed up his eyes and clenched his jaw-muscles, or beat his head lightly on the ground.

Not much point in watching Len the By-Product at the moment. Frankly, he's a dead loss from the light entertainment angle. Best to leave him to his own devices, and come back to him an hour or two later, at about the time that same storm is brewing which Mr Bleaker and Morgan are watching as they sit in the Inspector's room at Scotland Yard.

Old Len was on the move again, but the children had gone home, and the bathers had stopped bathing, most of them anyway, before Len stirred from the ground.

The air was still and oppressive as it had been for two or three days, but the sun had disappeared behind a bank of clouds, and this time the clouds were even more menacing than on the previous evening, so that it looked to Len as though the storm was really going to break this time.

Len stood up and ran his stubby fingers through his short, bristly hair, and walked to Hyde Park Corner. By the time he arrived at the Underground Station, the flashes of lightning were already playing on the horizon.

He bought a ticket for Ilford and went down to the trains.

Len Turner was on his way home, and his movements after leaving the train at Ilford are not without interest.

He did not know quite what he was going to say to Gladys,

or even precisely what he was going to do, but he knew he had to go home, if only to collect his clothes before leaving for ever. All kinds of thoughts, most of them painful, had gone through his head as he lay on the grass, so now he decided to turn in at the 'Feathers' public-house in order to try to sort them out and come to some decision.

A pint of best bitter beer would do him good and clear his brain. It would also give him some courage for what lay ahead. Good old Len did all his most profound thinking in public-houses.

He knew every pub in his home neighbourhood, and each had its own atmosphere and its own uses, according to his moods or needs. He was not a heavy drinker, but he liked public-houses, and that was all there was to it. The low murmur of voices, the occasional laughter, the smoky atmosphere, were soothing and enabled a man to figure out clearly his important problems, such as which dog to back, or where to go fishing the following Sunday. Also, he was well known in these places, and usually came across some chap he knew. He was welcome, too, and knew it, and liked the feeling.

Outside the 'Feathers' a newspaper vendor was selling the evening papers. One of his placards read: 'H-Bomb Test Sensation'. Len glanced at it, and went inside.

He was not at all concerned with H-bombs, or A-bombs, or bombs with any other prefixes, and regarded the activities of politicians as quite beyond his control, and therefore of no interest at all.

If a bloody war came – things were usually bloody to Len – then it came, and there was nothing he could bloody well do about it. So why worry? On the whole, he thought the Russians were a bloody menace and such Communists as he had met needed a kick up the backside for being crack-pots, and both occupied space in the newspapers which would have been better devoted to sport.

A kick up the backside had always been Len's sovereign remedy for everything from political extremism to a nervous breakdown, but that was before Gladys had let him down.

The 'Feathers' public-house was bleakly furnished, but its particular use lay in the fact that it was close to the Ilford

Underground Station, so that if one was in a hurry one could have a quick pint there on the way home.

Len was not in a hurry to get home, but he had a quick pint and left. The atmosphere of the place, though suited to certain purposes, was not snug enough. There were not enough people there that evening. He wanted somewhere where he could sit at a table in a corner and be soothed and think things out. He wanted the presence of others, the murmur of their voices, without the necessity to talk to them. He was feeling lonely, isolated in a treacherous world, and yet he did not want to mix socially with his fellow men.

He decided to try the 'Crown', a few hundred yards down the road, and had hardly opened the door when he regretted his choice. Stan Wilson was there, with Stan's wife, May, and Stan's brother-in-law. Stan worked at the power-station. One couldn't ignore Stan, especially when Stan was so obviously glad to see you. Stan said:

'Hello, hello, hello, here comes trouble! Good old Len! How's things? What're you having?'

'I'll have a pint, seeing it's you, Stanley,' said Len, in the mock patronizing way he affected on such occasions. There wasn't much else he could do. You couldn't refuse Stan. Stan would be hurt.

'You won't,' said Stan. 'It's May's birthday. You'll have a double Scotch, Len, and like it.'

He flung a couple of half-crowns carelessly on the counter and ordered the drink.

There wasn't much he could do about that, either. If it was May's birthday, and Stan wished to make a gesture, it would have been churlish to insist on a cheaper drink. Stan said:

'How's things, Len?'

'Fine, fine,' said Len firmly.

'How's Gladys?' asked May.

'She's fine, too,' said Len, picking up his glass. 'Well, cheers, and a happy birthday, May.'

'Haven't seen her for some time,' said Stan. 'You must bring her around for a bite to eat one evening.'

'That's right,' said May. 'Bring her around one evening.'

'What about next Sunday?' said Stan Wilson. 'What about that? Okay?'

'Don't know about next Sunday,' answered Len, gripping his glass tightly; 'got an idea we got something on, next Sunday.'

'What about Saturday, then?'

Len shook his head, said desperately:

'Got somebody coming ourselves on Saturday.'

'All right, then, what about Monday or Tuesday?'

Bloody hell, thought Len, they're going through every day of the week. But what did it matter? It would all be over, one way or another, in a few hours. He said:

'All right, Monday, then. I think Monday would be fine.'

'Six-thirty?' said May.

Len nodded, staring at the bottles on the shelf in front of him, not daring to look her in the eyes in case she suspected anything. He took a pull at his drink and said:

'Thanks, May. Six-thirty, Monday. Gladys will like it.'

Len drained his glass, pulled out his wallet, and began to extract a pound note. He said:

'We'll have another to celebrate May's birthday.'

He'd have to buy his round some time. Might as well get it over quickly. Buy his round and go. Find somewhere quiet to sit and think.

'Same again,' said Len to the barmaid.

'Not yet, you don't,' said Stan, putting his hand on Len's arm. 'George, here, has got to go in a minute. We got to sting old George for a round.'

'I got to go, too,' said Len.

'Not yet, you haven't.'

'I told Gladys,' said Len, and faltered.

'What did you tell her?'

'I told her I'd be back early,' said Len and swallowed hard.

Funny about Len, that evening. His emotions must have been very near the surface, otherwise one pint of beer and one double whisky, even allowing for the fact that he had not eaten, would have made little difference to him.

Stan Wilson soon disposed of Gladys.

'You can tell her it was May's birthday, and May only has a birthday once a year. Now then, George.'

So George bought his round, and then Len bought his, and then, to the surprise of everybody, May herself decided to make a gesture.

You couldn't very well refuse a drink from a lady on her birthday.

At ten o'clock Len said:

'I got to go now.'

'George has been going for the last hour and a half,' said May.

'Why?' asked Stan loudly. 'Why go now? It's not worth it.'

'I got to think,' said Len. 'I got to do some thinking.'

'Well, you'll think better after one for the road,' pointed out George, 'just one for the road.'

'Not for me,' said Len.

'Just a binder,' said Stan.

'One more to lace the others together,' insisted May, 'you'd do that for me on my birthday, wouldn't you, Len?'

It was all very well for May. She'd long since switched to orange-juice. She hadn't got to think, like Len, either. But oddly enough Len was no longer feeling at all maudlin. Moreover the pain in the stomach had died away.

Maybe he had been doing his thinking subconsciously, because he knew the answer now. It was perfectly clear. He'd got things into perspective. Gladys wasn't the first to slip up, nor the last, that's what the Inspector had said. And the Inspector was right. The Inspector was clearly a bloody clever man.

All Gladys needed was a good kick up the backside.

Good old Len the By-Product, the sucker, best to leave him while he's happy, this time. It's not a bad picture to remember him by. Len in his pub, surrounded by friends.

*

Otto Steiner has been watching the storm, too.

Unaware that his own legal adviser had taken a major step towards placing a noose round his neck, Otto Steiner sat at home at eight o'clock that same evening. The temporary feeling that he was, if not safe, at least in no immediate danger, had long since passed. He was reviewing his last interview with the police, recalling their questions and his answers, reading significance into certain of their questions, and thinking of how he might have expressed himself to better advantage.

He had reached the stage when he no longer tried to hide, even from himself, the fact that he was frightened and that he had just cause to be frightened. He feared the police, he feared for his family, and he feared, above all, the terrible loneliness of being put to death violently by alien hands in an alien prison.

He could hear Rose moving about upstairs, turning out and tidying some of the cupboards. Rachel was out with her *goy* boy friend. The thunder and the lightning had passed, and only the rain remained, falling steadily out of a grey sky.

At five minutes past eight, he adjusted his spectacles and began to glance at the Stock Exchange prices in an attempt to divert his thoughts. He held no shares, because all his money was invested in his shop, but he liked to keep abreast of the market. It was useful when talking to business acquaintants, and he had always hoped the day might come when he would be able to buy a few shares himself.

At a quarter past eight, he had a sudden urge to make a cup of coffee for himself and Rose. He got up and went out into the kitchen, filled the percolator coffee-pot, and came back to his chair in the bay window, although he never had a chance to sit down in it, because his heart began to throb so fast and so strongly, at the sight of the police car outside, that he almost choked.

He stood stock still, as two young men in plain clothes, whom he had never seen before, opened the small wicket gate, and came up the path, past the pocket-handkerchief-sized lawn, to the front door.

Otto Steiner was never much good in an emergency. He either lost his head or he remained frozen into immobility. He was that kind of man.

Right up to the moment when the bell rang Otto Steiner stood trying to calm the mad beating of his heart, and when eventually the sound of the bell shrilled through the house, he went to the other extreme and had to smother an almost uncontrollable impulse to run out of the house by the back door.

He heard Rose calling out, 'Who is that, Otto?'

When he did not answer, because he could not choke the words out, he heard the heavy sound of her footsteps as she made her way downstairs and to the door, and felt like shouting, 'Don't let them in, Rose! Rose, don't let them in; they are going to arrest me!' Otto Steiner was no longer captain of his soul, and never been had since the Hamburg terror.

If somebody had put a revolver into Otto Steiner's hand at that moment, he might have shot at the plain-clothes officers, or he might have shot himself, or he might have stared at the weapon and burst into tears. As Rose Steiner had remarked more than once, you couldn't tell what Otto would do in a crisis, not after the Nazis had finished with him.

In the present instance, when the men came into the room and told him that Inspector Morgan would like a word with him at the local police station, he reacted in a humdrum fashion, and this was right and proper, for Otto Steiner was essentially a humdrum type of man. It was only the world which had forced him repeatedly into situations with which he could not cope. So Otto Steiner gave a funny little gasp, and fainted, without further fuss, bother, or drama.

Meanwhile, Chief Detective Inspector Morgan sat in the barely furnished room in the Hampstead police station which had been placed at his disposal. He felt that the sooner the investigation was cleared up now the better for all concerned.

The case sickened him. He wanted to tidy it all up, and get on with some other job, a clean-cut case, where a bad man killed a good man, and there was satisfaction in bringing the criminal to book.

Morgan sat at the desk with his chin sunk on his chest, his face wooden and expressionless, glad that he had delayed his interrogation of Steiner until now, for now he had a motive for the crime in addition to some evidence. Meanwhile, two of his officers would be searching the Steiner house, and in particular they would be examining Otto Steiner's clothes for spots of blood or traces of petrol.

Shaw was with him, notebook ready open, and Shaw was

rejoicing inwardly. Shaw disliked and distrusted on principle everybody born on the Continent. He was not sadistic, but he liked a good verbal tussle with a foreigner, with no holds barred.

Morgan did not even look up when Otto Steiner was at length ushered in. It was not going to be a friendly interview and it was pointless to pretend that it was.

It was Sergeant Shaw who indicated where Steiner should sit. When Morgan eventually looked at Steiner he said, abruptly and without preamble:

'I want you to answer some questions as briefly and clearly as you can, although I must point out to you that you do not need to answer if you do not wish to. Understand?'

Otto Steiner swallowed, tried to speak, then contented himself with nodding his head.

'At our earlier talk, Mr Steiner, you said you had hardly ever seen this man Draper who was killed. You said that he left for work before you arrived, and arrived back after the shop had closed. You implied that you knew little or nothing about him. Was that correct?'

'Not entirely,' replied Otto Steiner in a whisper.

'You implied you had known him only since he came to live in Paton Street. Was that correct?'

'I didn't say that,' said Otto Steiner, in his soft, watery tone. 'I did not say that. I did not say I had only known him since he came to Paton Street.'

'You gave that impression, though, didn't you? Did you or didn't you? It's best to be frank, sir.'

'The Inspector's trying to help you,' said Shaw suddenly.

Otto Steiner nodded at Shaw. 'Yes,' he said. 'Yes, thank you.'

'Did you or didn't you give the impression you had only known Draper since he came to Paton Street?' persisted Shaw, tapping his teeth with his pencil.

'Perhaps I did.'

'Why?' asked Morgan. 'Why did you want to do a thing like that, Mr Steiner?'

Steiner shrugged his shoulders.

'I did not want to be pulled into the case.'

Sergeant Shaw laughed shortly, and looked at the Inspector as if to indicate that this was just the sort of silly answer he expected. He said:

'You didn't want to be dragged into the case! But you were in it already, weren't you? You didn't want to be dragged into it. That's good, that is!'

'How much longer than six months had you known Draper?' asked Morgan.

'A little bit longer.'

'Had you known him a year?'

'Maybe a year.'

'Or longer?'

'Maybe a little longer. Maybe a couple of years.'

'A couple of years? How did you get to know him?'

Steiner hesitated, pretending to search his memory, playing for time, for a few seconds to parry the question. At length he said:

'He helped a little with the business. Introducing customers now and then. You know?'

'How did you get to know him?' insisted Sergeant Shaw. 'We're not asking what he did for you, when he knew you – the Inspector is asking how you got to know him. Understand? Now then.'

'Have a cigarette?' said the Inspector unexpectedly, and pulled out his case. He offered Steiner a light.

An old trick, as old as the hills, but they always fall for it, thought Morgan. They think you are being friendly, until they accept the light. Then they see the cigarette trembling in the flame, telling everybody that they are frightened, and that they are probably frightened because they are guilty, and that disconcerts them still more.

Steiner watched his own cigarette wavering in the flame from Morgan's lighter, and sat back and looked at the Inspector with terrified eyes. I didn't need to do that, Morgan thought, and bit on his pipe, and told himself that the sooner the whole business was over the better.

'Well?' asked Morgan. 'How did you get to know him?'

Otto Steiner shook his head.

'I don't remember. One meets many people.'

'I should have thought you would have remembered quite well,' said Morgan coldly. 'I should have thought that that was one of the things in your life which you would never forget, sir.'

'If I say I don't remember, then I don't remember,' replied Otto Steiner, with a spark of resentment in his voice. 'You gentlemen cannot make me remember.'

'Why?' asked Shaw.

Steiner looked at him, astonished by the question.

'Why can't we make you remember?' asked Shaw. 'We've made lots of other people remember things. Why can't we make you?'

'You are not the Gestapo,' muttered Steiner uneasily, 'you do not torture people. You do not – '

'We're not so bloody silly,' snapped Shaw, 'we have other methods.'

'What other methods?'

'Reminding people of things,' said Morgan.

'Like what being frank and truthful is,' added Shaw, 'and what being shifty and dodgy is, see?'

Otto Steiner tried to smile.

'Well, if you will remind me of something – whatever it is – maybe I can help you. How do I know? I do not know. Perhaps I can, perhaps I can't.'

'You can, but you won't,' murmured Shaw, just loud enough to be heard.

Morgan put both his hands palms downward on the desk and looked at Steiner. Morgan looked bulky and solid at that moment. He gave the impression of being as immovable as a boulder, and almost as heartless. He raised both his hands and brought them down with a bang on the desk.

'How much were you paying Draper?' he said loudly.

'I don't understand.'

'Yes, you do, sir. How much? How much were you paying this chap Draper?'

Steiner stared at Morgan with his bewildered, uncertain expression.

'Why should I pay this Mr Draper any money?'

Morgan sighed, fighting down the feeling of compassion inside him. He had hoped it was going to be easy, but it wasn't. Yet he had to go through with it now, battering at Otto Steiner to get what he could out of him. That was what he was paid for, that was his job. You couldn't pick and choose your cases in the police force. Morgan said, calmly, almost conversationally:

'Look, Mr Steiner, you are wasting time, see? We know that Draper was blackmailing you, and if you had come to us in the first place we could have stopped it. But you chose to pay, instead. How much were you paying?'

'You know then about – ?'

He stopped, reluctant even now to bring the matter into the open, since to do so meant defeat.

'We know about your boy, Julius,' said Morgan, 'if that's what's holding you back.'

'And about the German Communist Party,' said Shaw.

'And about his job in America,' said Morgan.

'It is to be made public?' asked Steiner. 'Must it be made public? He is a good boy, Julius. No man had a better son than my boy Julius,' went on Steiner in a sudden rush of words. 'He has always worked hard and loved his parents; he is not a Communist, he never has been a Communist. He joined the Party in Hamburg, because he wanted to fight Hitler and the Nazi Party. He saw what they did to me, and to his mother, and to the business.'

Otto Steiner stopped and waved his arms excitedly, searching for words. He was pale now, and perspiring, and the sentences began to tumble over themselves in his excitement.

'He saw the Storm Troopers march to my shop, and throw the furniture into the street and break it up, and when I tried to stop them, they – '

Steiner buried his face in his hands, but the words came babbling out through his fingers, interspersed with sobs. Shaw made as if to speak, but Morgan silenced him with a movement of his hand. Better to let Steiner carry on, to allow the spate of words to pour forth uninterrupted.

Better to let the tears flow, to trickle through the spread fingers, and down the back of the hands, while he and Shaw sat and gazed at a bowed, bald head surrounded with grey hair.

Better, too, to let the sobs come out before they burst the over-full heart. Then there would be calm. Perhaps.

Steiner was no longer in Hampstead, no longer in the presence of two Scotland Yard officers. He was back again in Hamburg on the cold, bright November day when the Brownshirts descended upon him.

'The crowds, bigger and bigger and all in a circle round the shop. "*Heil Hitler! Heil Hitler! Heil, heil, heil! Juden! Juden! Juden! Heil, heil, heil!*" Like wild animals, howling wolves. . . . "*Heil, heil, heil, heil, Hitler!*" . . . They marched us out of the shop in the end . . . me and Rose, and Julius, who had called in from school. We had to go through them, we had to go through the crowds . . . they were shouting and spitting and jeering and throwing things at Rose and me, and always howling like wolves, "*Juden, juden, juden, heil, heil, heil, heil Hitler! . . .*"'

Rocking backwards and forwards in his hard chair, Steiner seemed to have forgotten all about Draper.

'They made me take my trousers off, and I was wearing the long woollen underpants which Rose makes me wear in winter, and I had a notice round my neck, saying "I am a Jew", and now and then they stopped us, and made us raise our right arms and cry "*Heil Hitler*", and once one of them made me raise my left arm too, and say "*Heil Hitler*" twice, and then touch my toes, and then he kicked me with his jackboot from behind, so that I staggered forwards and crashed to the ground and cut my forehead on a stone, and the blood ran down my face.

'I remember as I lay on the ground,' said Steiner, more calmly, 'I remember a little girl of about ten stepped forward out of the crowd and pushed past the Brownshirts, and spat down at me, and shrieked, "Death to the Jews!" She was blonde, a very pretty little girl, and I don't think she realized what she was doing. I shall always remember her little face all twisted with excitement and hate. I still have the scar here,' said Steiner, pointing to a short white line above his eye, 'I see it every morning when I look into the mirror to shave, and it reminds me.'

He began to wipe his spectacles and added: 'Please forgive me. I am very sorry.'

Shaw picked up his pencil and leaned forward. Morgan struck a match and relit his pipe. A woman, making a dash for shelter through the rain, ran past the police-station window, her high heels tapping quickly on the pavement. A man's footsteps followed, then another.

'Well, anyway,' said Shaw, 'how much did you pay Draper to keep his mouth shut about your son?'

Shaw, the practical, the stolid, thought Morgan, dismissing the hideous past in two words: well, anyway.

'Seven pounds a week, in one-pound notes, and a lump sum at first of five hundred pounds.'

'A pound a day,' said Morgan softly, and looked at Shaw.

'He asked me when he first saw me. "Mr Steiner," he said to me, "is it worth a pound a day to you to keep your son in his job, where he is doing so well?" At first I did not understand what he meant and then he explained. He said he was a reasonable man. "Some people in my position would ask more," he said, "but I am reasonable. I do not think you can pay more. I do not wish to ruin you and your business. It is better for me that the business should keep going. So, I will not ask more, Mr Steiner. Not at the moment, anyway. I am a reasonable man," that is what he said to me.'

'And now he is dead,' said Morgan, and examined the bowl of his pipe, 'so you don't have to pay him any more, and he can't talk. It must be a relief.'

'I would not wish a man to die like that. But – ' Steiner shrugged, and added: 'He was a hard man.'

'Did you ever ask him to reduce the payments?'

'Yes, I did.'

'When?'

'Recently. The shop had not been doing well. I asked him if he would take a little less. Just a little less, just temporarily. Till times got better. You know how it is?'

'What did he say?'

Steiner shrugged again.

'He said he was a reasonable man, but he had to pay the rent of his flat.'

'So you went on paying?'

'What else could I do?'

'You could have come to the police, for one thing.'

Steiner said sadly:

'You don't understand. You don't understand what was at stake. He is a good boy, my son. He has been spared to live and to work. After what we have been through, a pound a day for my son seemed –'

He broke off and looked at Morgan and at Sergeant Shaw, as though hoping they would finish the sentence for him. When they remained silent, he ended the sentence lamely, dragging the words out in his liquid, throaty tones.

'A pound a day seemed a price I must pay. I am not as young as I was. My wife and I, we have simple tastes these days. A book to read in the evening, a glass of beer, a visit to the pictures now and then. We are quite happy with those things. My children are both earning their living, Inspector. If it were not so, I would be paying much more than a pound a day. Why then should I not pay that sum to ensure that one of them remains in a good position?'

'You would have paid more in the end.'

'Perhaps. Who can tell? Things change. Julius might have changed his job, or things might have become easier in some other way.'

'Or Draper might have died, and did die. Is that what you mean?'

Otto Steiner said nothing. He adjusted his rimless spectacles, and looked at the Inspector with his soft brown eyes and remained silent. Morgan noticed a change in him.

In contrast with his earlier emotional outburst, he was curiously composed. The outburst had calmed him, as Morgan thought it would, but even Morgan was surprised at the change in him.

Steiner was alert and watchful now. He seemed to Morgan to be more cool and self-possessed than at any time since the outbreak of the fire. It was as though, in outlining the reasons why he had agreed to pay blackmail, he had suddenly convinced himself of the correctness of his actions, as though he suddenly saw all things in their right perspective, and regretted nothing that he had done.

Morgan said:

'How did it come about that Draper was able to live above you?'

'He told me to tell him if the flat was to be sub-let again.'

'So you did?'

'Of course,' said Steiner quietly. 'Although I did not like having him there. It was like, how do you say, rubbing salt into the wounds?'

'Why did he want the flat?'

Steiner raised a hand and let it fall again to his knee and replied:

'He said the neighbourhood suited him.'

'It was also convenient for collecting the money, no doubt. How often did you pay him?'

'Once a week. In one-pound notes, as I said.'

'And all the time, day in and day out, you saw him coming and going, and knew that he was the man whose extortions were threatening to ruin you. And when you asked him for some relief he refused it. And now he is dead,' said Morgan, for the second time.

'Yes, he is dead,' agreed Steiner, in his newly acquired detached way.

Once again Morgan had the impression that somehow, in some way, Steiner had suddenly acquired an inner strength which rendered him almost indifferent to the present investigation.

'As I indicated at the beginning, I am going to ask you some straight questions. You will understand that this is necessary, and that in a case like this one must – ' Morgan paused, choosing his words with care – 'one must take all steps to clear people one by one, so that one can then concentrate more closely on any that remain. You understand that?'

'Of course. Please carry on.'

'Did you visit Draper on the night he was killed, Mr Steiner?'

'Certainly not.'

'Did you visit his flat during the week or two before he died.'

'I did not,' answered Steiner, and turned his head to gaze

out of the window, as though the whole matter were no concern of his.

'How did you pay him, then?'

'I handed him the money in an envelope, as he left the premises to go to his place of work.'

'I see. Now I'm going to show you something.'

Morgan opened a buff folder on the desk in front of him, took out a photograph, and held it up so that Steiner could see it.

'Do you know what this is?'

Otto Steiner leaned forward in his chair to peer at the print.

'It looks like a photograph of a finger-print. What is that to do with me?'

'It's your finger-print,' replied Morgan. 'That's what it's got to do with you. Know where it was found?'

Otto Steiner shook his head equably.

'I expect I leave finger-prints in many places. Where was it found?'

'On the inside door panel of Draper's living-room,' said Sergeant Shaw sharply, 'that's where it was found.'

Otto Steiner frowned, and for a moment he looked as though he was about to protest.

'Did you increase the insurance on the contents of your shop recently?' asked Morgan, before Steiner had time to speak.

'Yes, I did. Have you any objections, Inspector?'

'Don't be perky,' snapped the Sergeant. 'The Inspector's asking the questions, not you. Don't go and get cocky with the Inspector because it won't do you any good, sir.'

'I increased the insurance by two thousand pounds.'

'When?'

'About two months ago, maybe three. I had increased my stock and – '

'Never mind about the reasons,' said Shaw. 'The Inspector didn't ask you about the reasons. He just wanted to know if you had increased it, see? If he'd wanted to know the reason, he'd have asked, wouldn't he, sir?'

Shaw was an adept at this sort of thing, he would smack a man down like a cross between a schoolmaster and a sergeant-major, and at the same time throw in an occasional 'sir' to make it difficult for the fellow to accuse him of bullying.

It had no effect whatever on Otto Steiner in his present mood.

'I was only trying to be of assistance,' said Steiner serenely.

'The best way to be of assistance is to stick to the answers to the questions the Inspector puts to you,' said Shaw, 'then we'll get somewhere. Otherwise we'll be all night, sir.'

'I have plenty of time.'

Shaw flung his pencil down, and banged the table.

'Well, you may have, but we haven't, sir! Is that clear?'

'It is as you wish,' said Steiner mildly, and took off his spectacles and began to polish them afresh.

Morgan was puzzled, and in a curious way disquieted.

Few people could stand up to Shaw when he was what he called 'showing 'em where they get off'. He was mystified because up to the point when Steiner had had his emotional outburst, he would have thought Steiner was the last person to be able to stand against the Sergeant.

He was disquieted, because he could not discover the reason for it. He was up against some imponderable, and while he was putting the questions and listening to the answers, he was vainly seeking for the source of Steiner's new-found strength.

It was not a positive strength, not an aggressive strength which leaped forward to attack when the opportunity arose. It was something negative yet resilient. Steiner bent before the blows of Shaw's onslaughts, and then recovered to where he had been before, but he went no further.

Steiner held an undisclosed card in his hand which was making him indifferent to the point of insolence. What that card was, and whether it was as strong as the man seemed to think, remained to be seen.

'Mr Steiner,' said Morgan carefully, 'tell me this, and please think carefully before you answer. Have you, within the last two weeks, bought any petrol loose, by which I mean, in a can as distinct from having it put into the tank of your car?'

'No, I haven't,' replied Steiner.

'Are you quite sure?'

'Oh, yes, I'm quite sure.'

Morgan, who had been puzzled and disquieted, was now irritated as well. Steiner was not even playing what cards he had with skill. He was tossing them down with a kind of impudent negligence, as if the winning or losing of a trick meant nothing to him.

'Look sir,' said Morgan harshly, 'I don't like lies, because we always find out the truth in the end, and lies waste my time. You've been less than frank with the police ever since we first spoke to you, and the Sergeant and I, we don't appreciate that kind of attitude. You've told one lie after another, haven't you, sir?'

'One bloody lie after another,' barked Shaw, reinforcing the point.

'It's a matter of opinion,' said Steiner. 'Doubtless you gentlemen have your own opinions on the subject.'

'They're not opinions,' snapped Morgan.

'They're facts,' said Sergeant Shaw.

'You may think –' began Steiner, but Morgan interrupted him.

'Listen to me, Mr Steiner.'

'If you insist.'

'When we first talked to you, you said you hardly knew Draper. Then after a lot of trouble, and when you couldn't deny it any longer, you admitted you had known him for two years, and that he had blackmailed you. That's one point.

'Secondly,' continued Morgan, ticking the points off on his fingers, 'you deny having been in Draper's flat for some time, but your finger-prints were found on the door-plate of the inside front door. Thirdly, you deny having bought any petrol in a tin, but I have here, in this folder, a statement by a garage mechanic that he supplied a man answering to your description, with petrol in a can approximately twenty-four hours before the murder.'

Morgan lifted the folder and banged it down again on the desk.

'What do you say about that last point?'

'I should say it is a case of a mistake being made,' said Steiner without hesitation.

'That remains to be seen,' said Morgan, and lifted the telephone receiver when the bell rang.

He listened for a few moments, said, 'I see, thank you,' and replaced the receiver. For some seconds he remained staring at the blotting-pad on the desk. Finally he said:

'Do you know a Mrs Wellings?'

'I do not know her, but I buy my cigarettes from her shop opposite.'

'She knows you by sight?'

'Certainly she knows me by sight.'

'She lives above her shop?'

'I believe so.'

'She was away when my officers made their first round of calls in connexion with Draper's murder. She is being interviewed at the moment. One of my officers has just telephoned me to say that she is making a written statement concerning you.'

'So?' said Steiner politely.

'Part of her statement is to the effect that she was sitting at her window on the night of the crime, because it was so hot, and saw you standing by the window in Draper's flat, looking down into the street. She says you stood there for about a minute, and then went back into the room. She had the impression that you might have been waiting for somebody to arrive. Have you anything to say about her information, Mr Steiner?'

Otto Steiner hesitated for ten seconds before replying.

During this time he looked at the fingers of his left hand. Morgan formed the impression that he was not so much disconcerted as thoughtful, occupied less with the nature of his reply than with the form it should take. He must have plumped for simplicity, because when he looked up and met Morgan's gaze, he said:

'I have nothing to say, except that it is true.'

'It might have been better if you had said so before, sir.'

'Instead of lying,' said Shaw. 'Lies, lies, lies, that's all we've had from you, sir.'

'The reason is simple enough. I don't think I need say it.'

'It might be better if you did,' said Morgan, and Steiner nodded.

'If you wish. I was afraid. At first, I was afraid that if you learnt of my association with Draper, and the reason for it, then the facts would be made public. And then – well, then I was afraid for myself.

'But now, tonight, in these last minutes, I am no longer afraid. Let me explain; it is not easy for you to understand, but I will explain.'

He leaned forward in his chair, his face a little flushed now, the eyes gleaming behind his spectacles. He passed his hand over his bald head thoughtfully, and muttered, 'I do not think you will understand,' and looked out of the window for a few moments.

'This is the way it is, gentlemen. While you have hope, you have fear, is it not true?'

But before he could proceed, the telephone rang again. And again Morgan answered it, and listened, and said, 'Thank you,' and replaced the receiver. But this time he made no mention of the nature of the call. Instead, he leaned back in his chair, and murmured:

'Go on, I am listening.'

'I was saying that while you have hope, you have fear, and then the phone rang,' said Steiner, with a trace of resentment in his voice.

'I can't stop the phone ringing, sir.'

'No,' said Steiner, seriously, 'no, you cannot stop the phone ringing. I know that. But it is so difficult to explain.'

'Have a try, sir,' encouraged Shaw, in an unusually gentle voice.

'While I thought I could keep my secret – or perhaps I should say my son's secret – I always had fear. You understand? Fear that Draper might not keep his word, fear that he might wish to keep his word but let something slip by accident, fear that he might ask more money than I could pay. Fear, even, that somebody else might remember about Julius and – cause trouble. Fear, fear, always fear. You understand?'

'Yes, sir, I reckon we can understand that part.'

'And then this man, this Draper, he was no longer alive, and

I was afraid that if I was questioned too closely – things would come out. I was afraid that something might be found among his papers, that anything might happen. Then nothing happened, nothing very much, and I began to hope. He was dead, taking his knowledge with him, and I had no more money to pay, no reason to fear him longer. So I began to hope. Then I began to fear about myself.'

He shrugged and added:

'It was silly, because I am no longer young. Whatever happened, my life had not many years to run. For myself, it was silly to fear, but one is human, is one not?'

'That's right, sir,' said Morgan.

Out of the corner of his eye, Morgan could see that Sergeant Shaw had lost interest and was playing with his pencil, trying to make it see-saw on his middle finger, fidgeting.

Shaw the Anglo-Saxon. No Celtic warmth, and not much sympathy in Shaw. He wanted to get on with the job, to stop all the Germanic introspection. For a second, Morgan wondered whether there were not, after all, two sides to Shaw's matrimonial difficulties.

He heard Steiner say:

'Then suddenly, when things seemed to be better, you have me brought here, and I learn all that you know, and I can see how things stand against me. So now I do not fear, because I do not hope.'

He spread his hands, palms upwards and added:

'I have done my best for my family. I examine my conscience, and I find that I have done my best. Perhaps I could have come to the police when Draper asked me for money. Perhaps I could have been more clever, more brave.'

'You certainly could,' said Shaw brutally. 'You've been a pretty good mug, if you ask me, sir.'

'But I did not ask you, Sergeant,' said Steiner, and smiled slightly. 'You see? I am almost rude, I do not even fear the Sergeant now.'

He looked at Morgan.

'But I think you understand,' said Steiner. 'It is said that only the man with no possessions is free. And so I think that in some cases only the man with no hope is free of fear. He is

– ' Steiner tapped his nose, groping for the word – 'he is resigned, I think you say.'

'And are you resigned, sir?'

Steiner hesitated and Morgan knew that he had told only part of the story. Steiner may have been speaking his views with some truth, he may have believed what he said, but the man was keeping something back. He had not entirely revealed himself.

Otto Steiner had shed his fear, thought Morgan, but he still had some hope left, if not for himself, then for his son, and therefore his argument was not completely true.

How or why he knew this, Morgan could not have said. It was part of that intuition, that fey streak in his make-up, about which he never spoke to his colleagues.

Steiner had put forth this argument for some reason best known to himself. But the real cause for Steiner's sudden accretion of inner strength lay elsewhere. Where, Morgan did not at the moment know. He would have given much to know. He still felt disquieted and puzzled.

'Look, sir,' he said, on impulse, 'I shouldn't be saying this to you, and I'm not putting pressure on you, and I'm not making what might seem to be an irregular suggestion, but in certain circumstances, and particularly if a chap has been cooperative, an English judge and jury will sometimes take a sympathetic view of a case.'

'The Inspector's not promising anything,' said Shaw quickly.

'I haven't got the power to promise anything,' said Morgan.

'He's talking off the record, if you know what that is,' said Shaw.

'It's just that in certain cases, a charge of manslaughter might be brought. Mind you, I'm not suggesting anything,' added Morgan.

'Manslaughter, not murder, that's what the Inspector means,' pointed out Shaw. And Morgan said:

'If, for instance, you quarrelled with Draper, and he happened to attack you, and you were defending yourself, and he got killed, there might be a manslaughter charge, or there might even be no charge at all.'

'It'd be your word against Draper's,' explained Shaw, 'and he's dead, isn't he? And he was a blackmailer. Not very popular characters with juries, blackmailers. Understand what the Inspector means?'

Morgan said:

'Even if you were charged with murder or manslaughter, you might be found not guilty. Juries are sympathetic to a chap who's been provoked like you have.'

'The Inspector shouldn't be talking like this, and if you repeat anything of what he's said, he'll deny having said it,' said Shaw, in a slightly threatening tone, 'and what's more, I'll say he's never said it, either. Get me? He's only trying to help you, see? So we don't want any monkey business later, and that's flat.'

'Well, sir,' said Morgan, after a pause. 'Is there anything you'd like to say? Any statement you'd like to make?'

'Are you going to arrest me?'

'We're not talking about things like arrests at the moment.'

'If I said I did not kill this man, you would not believe me.'

'I would take note of your remark.'

'We haven't much cause to believe what you say, at the moment, have we?' said Shaw. 'Not up to now.'

'What about the petrol?' asked Morgan.

'Do you still deny you bought it?' said Shaw. 'Do you still say this bloke is wrong when he says you did?'

'No.'

'No, *what*?' asked Shaw loudly. 'No, you didn't buy the petrol, or no you don't deny it any more? You want to make yourself plain, that's what you want to do.'

Steiner shook his head: 'All right, then – I did buy some petrol. And I've still got it in the back of the car, in a can.'

'You mean you've still got *some* petrol in the back of the car. But is it the same? – that's what we want to know. Or did you use the first lot to fire the flat, and then refill the tin? That's what you could have done.'

'I did not kill this man Draper, and I did not set fire to the flat,' replied Steiner stolidly.

Morgan sighed, and said:

'Now the final point. What were you doing in Draper's flat on the night he was killed?'

'Explain that one away,' said Shaw, 'go on, we're listening.'

Otto Steiner got up and walked to the window, and looked out, and stood for some moments watching the rain falling. Behind him, Shaw said:

'We haven't got all night, you know.' He began tapping his notebook with his pencil.

Steiner said, still looking out of the window:

'I had a key of the flat, because Mr Hitchcock, who owns it, he is a very particular man. He asked me to go up now and again to have a look at it, same as Mr Sylvester did, to see if it was being properly kept. I did not want to do it, but I agreed, because Mr Hitchcock has helped me – introducing customers to my shop, like I said Draper did, only he didn't. So I said, "Yes, all right, I will have a look in now and then." You understand? One good turn deserves another, I think you say.'

'So you went to have a discreet look round at just about the time when you would expect Draper to be at home or to be arriving home?' asked Shaw sarcastically. 'Is that what you're saying? I should have thought you could have thought up a better one than that. The Inspector, here, he won't believe that, you know. That's a bit thin, that is.'

'I didn't say I went for that purpose on that evening,' retorted Steiner patiently, and turned and went back to his chair. 'I did not say that, Sergeant, and you know I did not say it. No, I went up to wait for Draper.'

'Now we're getting somewhere near it,' said Shaw, and winked heavily and openly at the Inspector. 'Now we're getting at the truth of the matter.'

'Go on,' said Morgan, 'why did you want to see Mr Draper?'

'To ask him once again to let me pay him less – just for the time being.'

'And he said, no?'

'I never saw him. I never saw him at all that evening.'

'What time did you go to the flat?'

'I worked until about nine-fifteen, doing my accounts. Then I was about to go home. Very worried, I was. Then I thought,

"I will go up and show him my books, maybe I can prove to him with my books that what I ask is reasonable." So I went up hoping he was in. He was not there, so I let myself in, because I did not care by then whether he knew I had a key or not. I did not mind about that. I was too worried. I did not want to wait in my office in case he came in quietly and I might have waited longer than necessary. I wanted to see him, to talk, and then to go home and sleep. So I waited until about twenty-five past nine, and then I heard two people coming up the stairs and I thought it was him. But it wasn't. Somebody rang the bell. I did not answer, because I thought that if they were friends of Draper's they might wait, too, and then I should not be able to talk privately, to show him my books, my figures.

'So I waited, and the footsteps went away at last.'

'Are you sure there were two people, not one?' said Morgan.

'Quite sure. As they went downstairs, I went to the window, to see who it was. There were two men I did not know.'

'Surely he's not going to try that old one,' said Shaw in a low voice, but sufficiently loud to be heard by Steiner. 'Surely he won't try and pull that corny old story about the mysterious strangers who might have committed the murder?'

Steiner sighed.

'That is what I thought you would say.'

'How were they dressed?' asked Morgan quietly.

'One was wearing a grey suit and a light grey trilby hat. That is all I could see from my window,' explained Steiner. 'Looking down, and not taking particular notice, that is all I could see. I did not notice anything about the other one. He looked just – ordinary. Dressed in brown, I think.'

'And you've no idea who they might be?'

'No idea at all.'

'Then what happened.'

Nothing. I waited another ten minutes, and by then it was getting late, and I knew my wife would be wondering where I was. So I decided to speak to him on some occasion. "I cannot wait any longer," I said, and I went. That is what happened, but I do not think you will believe me.'

When the Inspector and the Sergeant remained silent, Steiner said:

'Do you believe me?'

'At the moment, we neither believe nor disbelieve anybody, sir,' replied Morgan.

'Then you do not believe me?'

'We will take a note of what you say, sir. The Sergeant here, he has taken a note in shorthand. It's all down in the book. But you are at liberty to make a written statement of your own, and sign it, if you wish to do so.'

Steiner shook his head.

'Mr Bleaker said – '

'You don't need to do everything that Mr Bleaker says, you know.'

'Nevertheless, I do not see that such a statement would help me.'

'It would show cooperation,' said Shaw. 'It would show you had nothing to fear or conceal.'

'I have nothing to fear in any case,' retorted Otto Steiner, and spread his hands again. 'As to concealment that can help me no longer. Will you tell me one thing?'

'Depends what it is,' answered Morgan cautiously.

'If I am tried for the murder of this man Draper – '

'There's no point in running ahead like that at this stage. I should – '

But Steiner interrupted him, eyes gleaming eagerly behind his rimless spectacles.

'This, you can answer. If I plead guilty, then there will not be evidence, is that not so?'

Morgan shook his head, quickly and emphatically.

'You don't want to depend on that. You don't want to rely on that at all. If anybody gets charged with murder, it wouldn't necessarily be any good pleading guilty just to prevent the motive from being made public. You don't want to reckon on that, sir.

'It might work, or it might not. It depends on the facts of the case, and on the judge. The judge, he might accept a plea of guilty or he might not. To be frank, sir, they don't often do it in serious cases like murder.'

Morgan was watching Steiner closely as he spoke, and saw the self-confident look fade in his eyes.

As the meaning of the Inspector's words sank in, Otto Steiner's inner strength seemed to seep out of him, leaving him as he was when he arrived at the police station, a badly shaken man, unsure of himself, unsure of the threats which still loomed over him and his family, the way ahead obscure and fraught with perils and difficulties.

'That will be all for this evening, Mr Steiner.'

The Inspector spoke suddenly and closed the buff folder in front of him. Shaw looked at him in astonishment. When Steiner had gone, he said:

'Was that wise, sir? You could have held him for twenty-four hours or so, while we checked up on whether this Hitchcock fellow really did ask him to keep an eye on the flat. He's a good liar, that bloke. A very plausible liar, he is. The dangerous kind.'

'We can pick him up again if we want him,' replied Morgan.

'Unless he tries to skip the country, sir.'

'He won't do that,' said Morgan, but Shaw, who knew him well, detected the undertone of uneasiness in his voice. 'He's got guts of a kind, Sergeant, you've got to give him that. It isn't everybody who'd try to plead guilty to a murder charge just to keep something quiet.'

'In my view, that was a bit of bolony, eyewash, sir. He's a good actor, is Steiner.'

Morgan sat silent, staring at the wall opposite, trying to persuade himself that he had acted correctly, that although he had a lot of evidence against Steiner, he hadn't enough to hold him and charge him.

'Anyway,' said Sergeant Shaw, following up his attack, 'even if what he said about pleading guilty was sincere, that's against him, too.

'A bloke who's got enough guts to plead guilty for a reason like that, has got enough guts to kill a blackmailer, and take his chance.'

'That's obvious,' answered Morgan impatiently.

'Yes, sir,' said Shaw, in a wooden dutiful voice.

Morgan was angry because he was grappling with the voice of his official conscience, because it was a losing battle, and because he thought Shaw might be right. He couldn't explain to him that he was delaying the arrest of Steiner till the last possible moment because he felt sorry for him.

It proved to be one of the most disastrous decisions of his career.

Chapter 7

GOOD old Len knew it had been thundering, but neither he nor the others had taken much notice of it, because among the clink of glasses and general noise in the 'Crown' the thunder had not sounded very loud.

But when the public-house closed, and they all began to drift out, the rain was cascading down in a continuous torrent. It wasn't so bad for Stan Wilson, and May, and George, because they only lived a little way up the road. They decided to run for it.

'It'll clear the air, anyway,' said Stan Wilson, putting up the collar of his jacket.

'That's right, it'll clear the air,' said May. 'So long, Len. See you Monday.'

'That's right,' said Len.

'Give my love to Gladys,' said Stan.

'Cheerio,' said George.

Then they were gone, scuttling up the road together, heads bent against the rain, Stan, and May, her high heels tapping on the pavement, and George puffing a few paces behind them.

Len watched them, saw them turn into their doorway, and hesitated in the entrance to the 'Crown', leaning against the door, wondering whether to wait in the hope that the rain would slacken, or start off on the half-mile to his house.

He decided to wait a few minutes.

They were the last out of the pub and behind him he heard the doors being closed and bolted. He continued to stand in the entrance, watching the falling rain. The street was almost empty, except for an occasional passing car, or a pedestrian, pressed for time, and hastening through the downpour.

A dog, a mongrel with a black coat and white chest and brown-and-white paws, came running along the pavement, stopped, looked round bewilderedly, ran on a little further, then came back towards Len.

The dog came up to Len, and sniffed briefly and glanced at him, and gave a short whimper, and ran on.

'Lost,' said Len aloud. 'Lost, poor bastard.'

He continued to stand watching the rain, and thinking vaguely of the dog, feeling sorry for the dog. He wondered whether the dog would find its way home, and considered, on reflection, that it looked thin and hungry.

He wondered how the dog had come to be lost. It was not a puppy. It looked fully grown. It ought to have known its own neighbourhood, its own way home.

But perhaps it wasn't in its own neighbourhood. Perhaps it had been brought there and turned adrift. You couldn't tell. People were funny like that, and other people and animals had to suffer for it. You got married and settled down and had a home and regular meals, like the poor bloody dog.

And you were all right. The kennel was warm.

You worked hard, brought a regular wage packet home, had an evening or two with the boys each week, went to a football match, did a bit of fishing on Sundays. Respected and liked by all concerned.

Nothing to worry about. No clouds in the sky.

Then suddenly you were adrift on the streets, like the mongrel in some ways, and it was raining like hell.

The drink that had cheered while others were present was now working against him. He was not drunk, but was not particularly sober, which was hardly surprising in view of the fact that he had had nothing to eat since his mid-day meal.

The temperature had fallen rapidly, and it was dark. There was no sign that the rain would stop. Sometimes it hurtled down in hissing sheets, sometimes it slackened a little and merely rained heavily.

There was no break in the sky, no wind to blow the clouds

away. The gutters were flooded, the water running in small rivers down the drains, gurgling as it went.

Lack of food and the sudden cool air made him feel chilly. He pondered upon whether to go and seek shelter with Stan Wilson, down the road, but decided against it, and pulled up the collar of his jacket, as Stan Wilson had done, and began to trudge along the pavement.

He was nearly home now, was Len. Not much longer. Once he said aloud: 'What about the brat?'

He didn't know the answer. If it was born, he'd either have to get it adopted, which would give the game away, or accept it in the home, and have it there for years, a living reminder of how Gladys had let him down.

At least he had got that far. He was going to try to forgive Gladys.

The light was on in the bedroom when he reached the house. He saw that at once, directly he entered the street. The living-room downstairs was in darkness.

He let himself in, and switched on the light in the little narrow hall, and went into the living-room. The place had not been tidied since the police had left. Cushions in chairs were crumpled, cigarette ends lay in the hearth, and also in the porcelain, gilt-bordered, little ash-tray with the brown dog's head, which he and Gladys had bought as a souvenir of a holiday in Worthing.

On the small side table was the Australian football coupon which he had been busily filling in when the police arrived. He went in for Australian football pools in the summer months, but of course it was during the winter months and the English season that he hoped to make his big coup.

He was always telling Gladys what they would do when they won £75,000. With life standardized and wages regulated and tabulated according to union rules, you had to rely on pools for colour and excitement and, above all, as background for your hopes.

He looked down at the half-completed coupon. The white paper dazzled him and he found it difficult to align the names of the teams. His head was heavy, and he was conscious of a feeling of dizziness, and put a hand to the upright piano to steady himself. Curiously, he felt more intoxicated now than when he had been with the others. In addition, he felt tired, very cold, and wet.

He made his way to the door, and along to the kitchen. He wasn't going to talk to Gladys until he had some food in his stomach. He wasn't going to give her the satisfaction of seeing him come straight up to her room. She could bloody well wait, the bitch. She could wait in suspense, and suffer a bit, the same as he had been suffering.

She had said, serve you damn well right, Len Turner, and he hadn't forgotten that, and never would. And it was going to be, serve you damn well right, Gladys Turner, and a scene she would never forget either. He was trying to whip himself into a rage, because it was better that way. It was less painful to be angry.

He opened the wire gauze of the meat safe, and pulled out a plate with some pieces of cold beef on it, and cut a hunk of bread, and spread butter on it, clumsily and thickly, and began to stuff pieces of meat and bread and butter into his mouth, sitting on the edge of the kitchen table.

His jacket and trousers were soaked, and his shoes soggy. Rain glistened on his hair, and the heat of the day, before the storm broke, had made his beard grow.

He sat chewing for five minutes, thought of making himself a cup of tea, but couldn't be bothered. Then he made his way along the passage and up the narrow staircase. At the top of the stairs he staggered slightly, and steadied himself with a hand on the wall, then he pushed open the door of the bedroom and strode in, saying:

'Now look here, Gladys – '

But Gladys had gone out, leaving the light on, and the room was empty and untidy. Some of her clothes were lying where they had been carelessly flung on to a chair, the bed was unmade; bedroom slippers and his dirty shirt of the day before littered the floor.

One way and another, it was a fairly sordid sight, but it didn't strike Len Turner that way, because each item meant something to him. The furry bedroom slippers had been a Christmas present he had given her the previous December.

She had only given him a cheap necktie, because she said she found it hard to save on her housekeeping money, and dress herself on it, too. He wasn't surprised now.

Len Turner, sitting on the edge of the bed in his damp clothes, thought she must have had to skimp and save quite a lot to be able to buy a wrist-watch for her lover.

It was good, that. Pretty ripe, that.

A wrist-watch for her boy friend, and a cheap necktie for her husband. They must have had quite a laugh about that.

'What did you give Len?'

'Just a cheap necktie,'

A laugh.

'Was he pleased?'

' 'Course he was pleased. Anything will do for old Len.'

'Good old Len.'

'He's pleased with anything I give him. He'd better be!'

Another laugh. Len, sitting on the edge of the bed, reckoned they must have had quite an amusing time talking about the necktie. Probably she had been sitting on his knee, watching him admire his new watch, while they joked about the necktie.

He jumped up and opened a drawer and took it out, and looked at it. It was green with a design of pheasants and – for some reason – foxhounds on it. As a tie for a charge engineer at a power-station in London, it was wonderful, thought Len.

She must have gone into a shop, pointed to the first tie she saw, and said, 'I'll have that.' A lot of loving care must have gone into the selection of that tie. Anything would do for old Len.

Len was slipping back into his nightmare jungle now, and the shrilly parakeets with scaly eyelids were mocking him again. Len was walking the treacherous paths, afraid of what he would see at each twist and turn, yet compelled to go on because he could not turn back.

Gladys going into that flat, while he, Len, was on night shift. Gladys lifting her face to be kissed, placing her plump arms round that man's neck.

Gladys calling him 'darling'.

Gladys calling him 'sweetheart'.

Gladys in his arms, voluptuous and ecstatic, then stealing

back home with a whispered promise, an agreed time and date to come again, to love again.

One way and another, it was surprising what Len found in his jungle, and he would probably have found a good deal more had not the front door below been suddenly opened and closed.

He had turned the lights out in the rest of the house, so she probably did not know he was back, probably remembered that she had left the bedroom light on. He heard her quick step on the stairs and then she came in.

She stopped dead when she saw him.

'I'm surprised you've got the nerve to come back,' said Len, not rising from the bed, 'but then I suppose you've got enough blinking nerve for anything.'

She pulled herself together, tossed her head, crossed the room without saying anything, and sat down in front of the dressing-table mirror.

He caught sight of her eyes glancing quickly at him in the mirror, calculating his mood, judging and estimating the way to deal with him. Cool, watchful, mentally on her toes, like an experienced cat faced with a large, excited dog.

No sorrow, no contrition, no tenderness in the eyes, only dislike.

'Where've you been?' said Len, loudly.

'That's my business.'

'And this is my bloody house!' shouted Len, getting up from the bed. 'You have got no right in this house now, my girl, and I got every right to sling you out, lock, stock, and barrel, bag and baggage. You got no right here now,' said Len again.

She had picked up a broken end of comb and was passing it through her fair hair. She said:

'You won't have to put up with me for long, Len Turner. So you can calm down, see?'

'Where are you going?'

'To my sister's, not that it's your business,' she replied, tugging viciously at a tangled lock of hair.

She said: 'You and me are finished, Len Turner, so you can get that into your thick head right now.'

She swung round from the mirror and glared at him.

'If you think I'm going to go on living here with you all the rest of my life, you got another guess coming. If you think I'm going to live here watching you glaring and sulking and insulting me, you're wrong, Len Turner!'

He walked over to her, underlip protruding, and hit her across the left cheek with the palm of his right hand. He saw the startled look, the flash of fear and pain in her eyes, as she instinctively raised her hand to her cheek. He raised his left hand to hit her on the other cheek, but she ducked away from him, and slipped off the stool in front of the mirror, and ran to the wall near the bed, and stood there, gasping and glaring at him, her back pressed to the wall.

'Keep away from me, Len Turner!'

He mimicked her:

' "Keep away from me, Len Turner – keep away from me, Len Turner!" You didn't say that to *him*, did you? Not bloody likely! You didn't say "keep away from me" to him, did you, eh? Eh? And look where it got you!

'A silver-wrist-watch for him, and a cheap bloody tie for me. Well, thanks very much, thanks for nothing, thanks for –'

She began to lose her own temper now, and that was silly, because cats faced with large dogs should always keep cool. It's their only hope. She said:

'He gave me more than you've ever given me, Len Turner.'

Len emitted some sort of noise that was supposed to be a sarcastic laugh.

'I bet he did, the dirty swine! And I bet he's given the same sort of things to lots of other cheap bints. You don't think you're the only one, do you? You don't think –'

But she interrupted him, almost beside herself with anger at the sneer in his voice and the insult behind his words.

'At least he was a gentleman and not a – a lout!'

He took a step towards her, his hand raised again, but this time she was ready and put out both her arms and pushed him back and to one side, so that the side of the bed caught him behind the knees and he flopped down.

She had lost her self-control completely now, and shouted at him as he floundered on the bed, which was a pity, both for her and for Len, because he misunderstood her words.

'And there's something else he's given me, which you never gave me, and you know what that is, don't you, Len Turner?'

She was waiting for him to ask what, and then she was going to say: 'A bit of human consideration, a bit of sympathy, see?'

But Len Turner didn't ask what.

Len felt his heart give a leap, and heard the blood pounding in his ears. He was still a little dizzy with drink. Looking up from the bed, the bright ceiling light dazzled him so that he found some difficulty in focusing her face; but not so much difficulty that he couldn't see the sneer on it, or imagine the sneer on it.

The inability to have children had always been a sore point between them. Each had been inclined to blame the other.

So now Len Turner misinterpreted her words, found an insult where none was intended, and turned very pale, and rose slowly from the bed.

Gladys had never seen Len turn quite as pale as that, nor stare at her so fixedly, nor move so slowly when he was angry.

She couldn't understand why he had suddenly gone funny like that.

*

Gwen Morgan knew that something was wrong with her husband directly he arrived home. He made the usual inquiries as to what she had been doing, but in a perfunctory manner, nodding his head absently when she replied, offering no comments of his own.

Just before they went to bed, she went out and made the cup of tea which they always drank before retiring for the night. It was at this time, especially, that Morgan would relax and talk to her of his worries, lighting a final pipe, and leaning back in his chair with his cup of tea, his face, lined but calm, lit by the standard lamp at his side.

She always enjoyed this evening chat, and would look at him, and think how solid and squarely built he was, and listen to the occasional Welsh lilt in his voice, and feel safe and secure.

But tonight he said nothing. He sat quietly stirring his tea, sipping it, looking into the empty grate.

On the principle that a minor worry might temporarily distract his thoughts from a greater one, Gwen Morgan said:

'I had Monica Shaw round here today.'

Morgan looked up.

'What did she want?'

'She wanted to know whether I thought she would be justified in leaving your Sergeant in favour of another man,' said Gwen Morgan calmly.

Morgan stared at her anxiously.

'What did you say?'

'I said she wouldn't.'

Morgan frowned and took a sip of hot tea.

'Monica Shaw is a slut,' he remarked dispassionately. 'She's married to a chap who, in spite of his limitations, is still one of the best sergeants at the Yard –'

'That's what she complains of. She says she might just as well be married to a Scotland Yard desk.'

'She keeps her flat like a pig-sty,' remarked Morgan. 'And she treats Fred Shaw as though he was a naughty schoolboy.'

'She says she hasn't any incentive to keep it nicely. She says he doesn't show her any sympathy for all the hours she's alone, she says he is quick-tempered, and only interested in his job, and takes her for granted –'

'And so on, and so on,' said Morgan. 'I seem to have heard all that before. Who's the other chap?'

'She didn't tell me his name. He's an instructor at some swimming-baths or other.'

'She wants to leave Fred Shaw for a swimming instructor?' said Morgan in utter astonishment. He gave a groan and put one hand to his head. 'What's he specialize in, the side stroke, or the backstroke, or – ?'

'That's quite enough, Dai, *bach*! I advised her to give her marriage another six months. She agreed. She's a good little thing at heart, but Fred Shaw ought to make more of a fuss of her. If he's going to go on treating her like a piece of furniture –'

'I'll see he gets some leave, once this confounded case is over.'

'And you'd better give him a good talking to, too,' said Gwen.

'I'll see about that,' replied Morgan cautiously. 'It's tricky, that sort of thing. I'm a policeman, not a welfare officer.'

'He'll take notice, if you tell him, Dai. He admires you.'

'I'm not promising. It'll have to wait till this case is over,' said Morgan.

He fell to thinking that people didn't realize that police officers had private lives, domestic difficulties, office squabbles, that one or the other might seriously interfere with their work. They saw well-built men with calm manners, and expected them to be always on duty, twenty-four hours a day, day in, day out, and never to suffer from ruffled nerves.

'They take it all for granted,' muttered Morgan, commenting aloud on his thoughts.

'What do they take for granted?' asked Gwen.

'Oh, everything,' replied Morgan vaguely.

They could never imagine that a police officer might conceivably feel a sense of compassion which could cause him to make a wrong decision.

Shaw would have detained Otto Steiner for further questioning. But Shaw was involved in a vicious circle. His unhappy domestic life caused him to regard his work as the mainspring of his life, which in turn made his relationship with his wife unhappier still.

Shaw had perforce to pull down a shutter against any human emotions he might feel for fear of suffering too much himself. He had to encase his heart in a kind of protective shellac covering.

One day, somebody might melt the covering, and then Shaw would be fit for human consumption. If it wasn't Monica, it would be some other woman. Morgan didn't give a damn who it was, so long as it was done. Then Shaw, too, would be able to make a mistake in a case involving a man like the wretched Otto Steiner.

But had he made a mistake? He still believed Steiner might be innocent. His men had found no blood or petrol on Otto's clothes, and had telephoned him at the police-station to that effect, and what Steiner had said about the callers tallied with what Miss Bellamy had told him she had seen through her binoculars. But the Callers, as he now referred to them, were probably, quite innocent people.

He realized he could not be obstinate about it much longer. He went up to bed, thinking: I'll give him twenty-four hours, and see if something turns up in the meanwhile.

In bed, he tried to read, but after ten minutes he gave it up as hopeless. He was unable to concentrate, because try as he might he could not help thinking of Shaw's words: 'Was that wise, sir? . . . A very plausible liar, he is. The dangerous kind. . . . Eyewash, sir. . . . He's a good actor, is Steiner. . . .'

Shaw was a very hard-headed man, objective, and in his present mood unswayed by humane feelings. Morgan shook his head, angry with himself, and angry with Shaw for probably being right.

He sat up in bed and reached for the telephone, and dialled the number of the Central-Exchange News Agency, and asked to be put through to the Night News Editor. Morgan looked at his watch and said:

'This is Chief Detective Inspector David Morgan of New Scotland Yard. I should regard it as a favour if the following message could be sent to all national newspapers for the favour of insertion in the midnight editions, if possible, or if it is too late for that, in the London editions.

'The police are anxious to establish the identity of two men who called at Number 127, Paton Street, at about 9.30 p.m. on the evening of June 5th. It is believed that these men could be of assistance to the police in connexion with the investigation of the murder of Robert George Draper.

'One man is described as about 5 feet 8 inches in height, of medium build, and was wearing at the time a grey-coloured suit, and a light grey soft hat. The other man was of medium build and wearing a brown suit.

'Will the men concerned, or anybody who may have seen them, or who may know of anybody who announced his intention of calling at 127, Paton Street, please communicate at once with New Scotland Yard, telephone number, Whitehall 1212, or with any police station.'

For a few seconds he thought of sending a patrol car to pick up Steiner and hold him for further questioning. But to do so would be a blatant admission of error.

Twenty-four hours, he thought again; I'll give him twenty-four hours.

Chapter 8

THURSDAY, June 8th was a day which Chief Detective Inspector Morgan would never forget.

The rain had ceased but the sky was still grey when Morgan left his house. He had to make a detour on the way to the Yard, in connexion with a manslaughter case he had been handling before the Paton Street murder. It was not until he arrived at the Yard that he heard the news.

Shaw had dealt with the matter before Morgan arrived, and broke the news in his usual phlegmatic way.

'That bloke Turner, husband of Gladys Turner,' said Shaw.

'What about him?' asked Morgan, putting his hat and gloves on the top of a steel cabinet.

'He's strangled his wife,' said Shaw. 'With a tie. He's given himself up. He asked for you, but I saw him instead. He looked as if he'd been walking about all night. When I went down to him, he just said, "I done her in", and tossed down a tie with pheasants and dogs patterned on it. That's all he said, "I done her in". Inspector Chapman is up at the house now. He's just been through on the blower.'

Morgan sat down slowly in his chair.

'I thought he looked a bit queer when he rushed from the house,' added Shaw. 'Still, I didn't think he'd go that far. You can't tell, can you?'

'Has he made a written statement?' asked Morgan heavily.

'Yes, sir. And he's been charged. When charged, he replied, "All right, get on with it." '

'I see.'

'If he'd let you see her alone, sir, as you suggested, it'd never have happened. He kind of rushed to destruction, that bloke did,' said Shaw, with unusual eloquence, 'like those pigs in the Bible.'

'Does Chapman want any help from us?'

Shaw shook his head.

'It's a straightforward enough job, sir.'

'I can't help feeling sorry for that chap,' sighed Morgan.

'Yes, sir,' said Shaw respectfully. 'Not that there's many women I'd swing for,' he added belligerently. 'Let 'em get on with it, that's what I say. Let 'em get on with it!'

'It's not a thing to say too loud or too often, Fred,' remarked Morgan, and looked out of the window to let the remark sink in. He was rather proud of it. He thought Gwen would have approved.

'Four things, sir,' said Shaw after a pause. 'There's another anonymous postcard.'

The Inspector reached out his hand and took it. It was in the same handwriting as the first one, and posted in London as before. The date stamp showed 6.30 p.m.

It said:

SEE WHO HAS LEFT LONDON SUDDEN.

Morgan tossed it on to his desk impatiently.

'That's helpful, that is. Check the population of London, and see who's left London suddenly, will you?'

Shaw said: 'There's a young woman downstairs called Alice Tamworth, from Lincoln. Wants to see the officer in charge of the case.'

'Who the hell is Alice Tamworth?'

'Says she's Draper's fiancée, sir. Can you beat it? And there's a bloke who won't give his name, but says he came as a result of what appeared in the morning papers.'

Morgan made a sound which was a cross between a laugh and a snort.

'It's a funny thing about some of these cases, Sergeant. You go scratching around for ages and can't pick up a thing, and then suddenly the floodgates seem to open, as it were, and you get almost more than you can deal with.'

'And Mrs Wood telephoned about Wood alias Draper's will, if any, and property. She wants to go through his papers.'

'Well, she can't, not yet. Send the girl up to me, and you see if you can get anything out of this other bird. Anything he may have to say about the Callers is worth having. Anything.'

Shaw was looking at him with a curious expression on his face.

'What's the fourth thing?' asked Morgan, conscious of a sinking feeling inside him. He saw Shaw hesitating.

'Go on,' he said, 'what is it?'

'It's about Otto Steiner, sir. He's skipped.'

'Skipped?' repeated Morgan foolishly.

'That chap Bleaker tried to get hold of him at his shop, and found he wasn't there, and rang up his home. The daily help said Steiner and his wife had left some money and a note for her in an envelope. The note was written last night. It said they had been called away unexpectedly late yesterday evening, and wouldn't be back for some days. I've alerted all police forces, and warned all sea and air ports to watch for them, and detain them should they try to leave the country. I trust I did right, sir?'

Morgan nodded.

'I'm afraid – ' began Shaw, and stopped.

'So am I,' said Morgan bitterly.

'I've asked all ports to check whether they have already left the country by normal routes. We should know soon, sir.'

Morgan began to fill his pipe, slowly and methodically. Strangely, he was conscious of a feeling of injury, rather than one of anger.

Shaw had been right.

Shaw the Anglo-Saxon, the unimaginative one, who based his reasoning on facts, had been vindicated.

Steiner had skipped.

Steiner, the very plausible liar, the dangerous kind. Steiner, the good actor.

Steiner had skipped.

The pathos about the Hamburg persecutions, the tears, the suggestion that he might plead guilty to save his son, these were all part of the act.

Bolony, Shaw had said. Eyewash. And he had fallen for it.

He applied a match to his pipe. He remembered how he had

toyed with the idea of ordering a patrol car to go along and pick up Steiner at his home. Compassion had stayed his hand, a desire to be sure before striking had caused him to waver, and pride had prevented him from rectifying the error. That's the way it had gone.

They would pick him up in the end. That was inevitable. Sooner or later, as sure as night followed day, some police force would be sending a message to say that they had him. The whole incident was so – futile.

Pity, a tendency to give a man the benefit of the doubt, to be swayed by his past history, by a hard-luck story, were weaknesses for which there could be no room in a police officer's make-up. After all his years of experience, he realized that he should have known that.

When he had let Steiner go home after the interrogation, he had felt that, although nothing was said to suggest it, he was in a way releasing Steiner on parole, and that Steiner had understood this.

The parole had been broken, and he had only himself to blame. Steiner had panicked. He had seen himself, as he was, the stranger in a strange land, despite his naturalization, despite the refuge which had been given to him in his hour of need. He was a German by birth, he was a Jew, he was surrounded by alien people in an alien land, his nerve weakened by earlier brutalities, by blackmail, by the ever-present threat to his son's livelihood.

Pressed beyond endurance, he had struck his blow, and thereafter the instincts of self-preservation had taken charge. He had lied plausibly, he had acted well, and, as Shaw put it, he had skipped.

'He may have done a bunk, even though he's innocent, sir. People get wind-up sometimes.'

Shaw letting his superior down lightly; trying to paint things in a better light.

Shaw being tactful, for once.

'Would a jury believe it?'

The Sergeant remained silent.

'I reckon I've put up a bit of a black this time, Fred.'

'We all make mistakes, sir. Now and then.'

'You wouldn't have made this one, would you?'

'Well, sir – '

'What about that daughter of his?'

'I got her on the phone, sir. She said it was the first she had heard of it. She says she was on night duty. She seemed distressed, sir.'

Morgan roused himself.

'There's not much doubt now about things, is there?'

'Well, sir – ' began Shaw, but Morgan shook his head.

'Send this Alice Tamworth creature up. And you see the other bloke, as I suggested. I don't think the Callers have got much significance now, but we'd better clear up their identities, if we get a chance. It's the sort of bloody thing the defence will pick on, unless we can find them.'

For Chief Detective Inspector David Morgan, the Paton Street case was as good as closed. It was all over bar the banging, and the noose was going to be round Otto Steiner's neck.

Shaw left the room, and shortly afterwards there was a knock at the door and Alice Tamworth was shown in. Aged about twenty-eight, thought Morgan. Small and slightly built. Pointed nose and chin, small mouth, thin lips. Grey, shrewd eyes, light brown hair, artificially crinkled. Dressed in a green frock; white hat, white handbag, and white shoes. Heavily made-up with a good deal of rouge on the high cheek-bones. A different type from the full-blown Gladys Turner. Draper clearly went in for variety.

'I was Mr Draper's fiancée,' she said succinctly.

'You were?'

'So you can imagine it came as a proper shock to me to read about what happened to him.'

She was smoking the cigarette Morgan had given her when she sat down. She was quite composed. He reckoned that if she had had a weep over Draper's fate, it was a short, sharp one, now long since past.

'We were going to be married in the autumn,' she added.

'You were?' said Morgan again. 'How long had you been engaged, Miss Tamworth?'

'Eighteen months,' said Alice Tamworth crisply. 'Quite long enough, too. Now I've come to know if you will help me.'

An extrovert, a down-to-earth type, thought Morgan. Not one to cry over spilt milk or dead Drapers.

'And how can we help you?'

'I want to get in touch with his family. Not now, of course, it wouldn't be decent, but later, after the inquest and funeral, and all that. Bob always said that if anything happened to him, he'd made arrangements to see I was all right. Understand what I mean?'

'I think so. Had you met any of his family, Miss Tamworth?' She shook her head, exhaled some smoke.

'I'd never met any of them, not actually met them, but of course I knew all about them.'

'Oh, of course.'

'I expect you've had a word with his father, haven't you?' she asked.

'Not yet,' replied Morgan, carefully.

'He's the owner of a big engineering firm in Ilford. Bob said he must be worth half a million.'

'It's a lot of money,' said Morgan.

'Bob did all the work, though. He was the brains of the outfit since the old man retired.'

'I believe he was very clever in his own line.'

'But the old man was mean, that was the trouble. Hardly paid Bob a living wage. You'd hardly credit it, would you?'

'No, you wouldn't,' said Morgan.

'But Bob didn't mind, because the old man had a dicky heart, and as I said to him, "Just be patient, Bob," I said. "Don't go and quarrel with the old geezer, or he'll cut you off without a sausage. Hang on, and you'll get the lot. Mark my words," I said, "you'll have the last laugh yet." I couldn't tell this was going to happen, could I?'

She began to fumble in her handbag, and eventually brought out a letter.

'I've got one of his letters here, in which he says that whatever happens I'm going to be all right. He also mentions a diamond ring he's been having specially made for me in London. I'd like to have that, naturally. Just to remember him by, of course.'

'Of course.'

136

'Plus the money I've spent collecting my trousseau together, and any special arrangements he'd made for me. I want to go into that, too, when the proper time comes.'

She put the letter back into her bag and snapped it shut. Morgan said:

'What else did he tell you about his father?'

'Nothing much. Except that he kept a yacht, and Bob and I would go for cruises in the Mediterranean. Also that the old man expected to be given a baronetcy one of these days.'

'He did?'

'He was offered a knighthood after the war, for his services.'

'Was he indeed?'

'But he turned it down. Bob said he knew he'd get a baronetcy in the end.'

'Then you would have been Lady Draper one day?'

'That's what Bob said,' replied Alice Tamworth, and added briskly, 'well, it's no good moping, is it? What's gone is gone, eh?'

'Now you want to try to salvage something from the wreckage, is that it?' asked Morgan.

'You could put it that way. But not till after the funeral,' added Alice Tamworth primly.

Draper, the clerk in a firm of bookmakers, pretending to be the clever son of a wealthy man and destined for a baronetcy – this could have been tragic, thought Morgan, and was thankful that Alice Tamworth was the type she was. There was going to be an almighty explosion when she learnt the truth, but no broken heart.

'Can you think of anybody whom Mr Draper had quarrelled with, anybody who might have wished to do him an injury, Miss Tamworth?'

She shook her head, and stubbed out the remains of her cigarette in the ash-tray on Morgan's desk.

'He never discussed his friends with me, or his enemies, if he had any. I asked him once or twice, but he said he was a kind of lone wolf.'

'A very apt description.'

Morgan got up and walked to the window and stood looking out, watching a barge chug its way slowly past.

'Miss Tamworth, are you sure he mentioned nobody of whom he might have been scared?'

'Of course I'm sure; I would have remembered it, if he had.'

'Didn't it strike you as a little odd that he said he had made some sort of provision for you in case anything happened to him?'

'I remember telling him not to get morbid.'

'It was almost as though he had a premonition that something was going to happen to him, wasn't it?'

'Well, anyway,' said Alice Tamworth, 'he never mentioned anybody to me, so that's that.'

Morgan heard the internal telephone ring behind him, and picked up the receiver. Shaw said:

'I think you'd better pop along and see this gentleman, sir.'

'Now?'

'Yes, sir.'

'All right – ' Morgan paused. 'And Shaw? I think you'd better pop along and see this lady. Tell her what we know about Mr Draper. I think she'll be interested.'

'What do you know about Mr Draper?' asked Alice Tamworth, suddenly suspicious.

'The Sergeant will explain,' said Morgan, and thanked her for calling, and eased himself quickly out of the room. He felt that Shaw was better equipped to deal with explosions at the moment.

He met Sergeant Shaw in the corridor, explained briefly the position in regard to Alice Tamworth, and asked about the man in the waiting-room.

For once, Shaw was evasive.

He gave Morgan a queer, thoughtful look, and contented himself with saying:

'You'd better hear his story yourself, sir.'

'Meaning what?' asked Morgan uneasily.

'You'd better form your own opinion, sir. His name is Harry Perkins, and he's employed by Joe Parsons, the bookie chap mentioned by Ed Tilling, if you remember.'

'The man whom Draper owed money to, and whom Tilling

said was one of the ones who wouldn't mind if Draper broke his neck?'

'That's right, sir.'

Morgan nodded, and passed on down the corridor, and downstairs to the waiting-room where Perkins was waiting.

Mr Harry Perkins was a thick-set man with a large stomach, a bald head, and a walrus moustache. A gold-coloured watch chain was stretched across his waistcoat, from one pocket of which a number of pens and pencils protruded, fixed into the pocket of clips of varying sizes and shapes. His face was red, and there was a large pimple on the end of his bulbous nose. He was the type of man who, when called up in the 1914–18 war, invariably wangled himself a cushy job in the quarter-master's stores. He had large, brown, knowing eyes.

A good friend, so long as you played along with him, flattered him, pandered to his pride and vanity. A man who liked to regard himself as a 'bit of a character', an Old Sweat; a scrounger, who would amass odd bits of equipment which he would flog to recruits for personal profit. A good ally, if you played ball with him, but a wicked enemy.

Perkins moved in to the attack almost before Morgan had closed the door.

'Now look 'ere,' he said firmly, 'I don't want to get mixed up in this 'ere business, and I don't want no come-back from Joe Parsons, when he turns up again. As I said to the young sergeant-chap who was in here, I said – '

'It's all right, Mr Perkins, we'll keep you out of it if we can, and if we can't – '

'Now, look 'ere,' said Harry Perkins again, 'there's no question of "if you can't". I got my reputation, I'm known where I live, I'm secretary of the British Legion Branch, and assistant treasurer of the Ex-Servicemen's – '

'You can talk quite freely, Mr Perkins.'

'I can,' retorted Harry Perkins triumphantly, 'but the point is, will I? I got to be assured – '

'You can rest assured that unless you are required to give evidence on oath in the witness-box, your information will be treated as confidential.'

'I'm prepared to do my duty, if so required,' said Harry

Perkins, 'same as I did in 1914, and again in 1940 when I was an air-raid warden, in spite of my rheumatism. Nobody's ever accused me of not being willing to do my duty, as and when the necessity arose.'

Perkins droned on for two or three minutes about duty, air-raids he had experienced, compliments paid him by people of national importance, and tributes he had earned locally by his selfless and unremitting toil for disabled ex-servicemen. A bore in the home and out of it, thought the Inspector, and probably a petty tyrant as well, a man who indulged in charitable activities for reasons of personal vanity, a busybody and a pest, a conversational menace in the saloon bar, where he would allow toadies to buy him beer, and yet with it all, a knowledge-able fish in a small pond, the type one had to listen to.

Morgan waited patiently. When a suitable pause occurred he said:

'I believe you wish to tell us something, is that correct, Mr Perkins? Perhaps you would repeat to me what you have told the Sergeant.'

'Joe Parsons is all right,' began Perkins, wagging his finger solemnly. 'I'm not saying anything against Joe Parsons as a guv'nor. He's always played straight with me, because he knows he can trust me. Five years ago, almost to the day, when I first went into his office to help with the books, he said, "Mr Perkins," he said, "I want a man I can trust in this job. I don't want nobody who'll fiddle the books, I want an honest man." '

'Oh, God, no,' groaned Morgan to himself, not more of it, not more about the wonders and integrity of Harry Perkins. He said hastily:

'I think you came along in response to an appeal which appeared in the newspapers?'

Perkins nodded heavily, and stroked his walrus moustache.

'That is correct. I considered it my duty so to act. Mind you,' said Harry Perkins warningly, 'I can only say what I know. I can't do more than that, can I? And I know that on the afternoon of the day when this 'ere Draper bloke was killed, I heard Joe Parsons ring him up and say he was going around that evening to collect the sixty-seven pounds, ten shillings and ninepence, that being the sum Draper owed him for betting losses. And if he didn't have it, it would be the worse for him. That's all I know,' said Perkins with an air of finality. 'That, and the fact that Joe Parsons is a hot-tempered man. Fair, mind you. Fair-minded, get me? But hot-tempered. He'd blow his top, and then it'd be over, see? Mind you, I won't hear a word against Joe Parsons, but duty is duty, and in view of the bit in the newspapers –'

'You acted correctly,' said Morgan hastily, 'but isn't it unusual for a bookmaker to call in person, and –'

He left the sentence unfinished.

'Ah!' said Perkins, brown eyes gleaming, 'but Joe Parsons, he knew Draper personally, that's what made it different, see? That's why he got so shirty about it. He give Draper more credit than he would have done to other blokes, see? And Draper let him down, took advantage, you might say. Draper, he'd worked for a while for Joe, and then left to better himself, so to speak. Ed Tilling, he offered more money. So he left, and no hard feelings on either side, not at that time. "You go, if you can get more dough," Joe Parsons says to him. "You go, Bob, me lad, and good luck to you." Joe's all right, in that way.'

'And then?' asked Morgan mechanically, but he put the question to keep Perkins talking, to give himself time to allow his thoughts to range around the idea which was forming in his mind, rather than from any particular desire for an answer.

'Then old Bob Draper, he started betting regularly with Joe Parsons. He said if he was going to lose money, he might as well lose it to somebody he knew than to somebody he didn't. At first he won a bit, then he lost – the usual thing.

'Then he started betting quite heavy,' said Perkins, fiddling about with his watch-chain. 'But he always paid up. He said he'd been left some dough by an aunt. Then recently he couldn't meet his losses. At first Joe let him run up quite a bit of credit. Joe's all right that way. But when he got to owing him over fifty quid, he began to smell a rat, began to get a bit nasty. It's natural. He knew Bob Draper was living in this flat, and he said to me, he said, "If Bob Draper can go on living in a flat like that, he can damn well pay me what he owes me, even if it's only a bit at a time.'' That's what he said.'

'What was he wearing that evening?' asked Morgan urgently. 'Can you remember that?'

Harry Perkins leaned back, thumbs in the armholes of his waistcoat, giving an exaggerated performance of a man thinking hard.

'Yes,' he said frowning, 'I am able to tell you that, Inspector. He was wearing a grey tweed suit, a cream shirt, and his green tie.'

'Any hat?'

'He always wore a light grey hat. He never went out without that, he didn't.'

So that's that, thought Morgan, and felt the wave of uneasiness, born when Perkins was telling his story, begin to surge through his nerve-centres. It tallied with Miss Bellamy's description, and it tallied with Steiner's description. Steiner couldn't have invented it.

Steiner waiting in the flat to plead with Draper. Hearing the bell ring. Not answering, because he wished to be alone with Draper to make his last appeal to Draper's non-existent humanity.

Steiner with his account books, letting Joe Parsons ring and go away. Joe Parsons was one of the Callers all right. If Steiner was telling the truth about that, he might have been telling it about other things.

'And did he get the money when he called?' asked Morgan at last.

'Ah,' said Harry Perkins significantly, 'that's just what we don't know, see?'

'Why not?' asked Morgan, though he thought he knew the answer before Perkins said it. He thought he knew, also, who wrote the anonymous postcards.

'Because he ain't been back since Draper was killed, that's why,' said Harry Perkins. He was looking at the Inspector in a stolid way, to hide his pleasure at being able to make what he considered to be a dramatic announcement.

But Chief Detective Inspector Morgan, surprisingly, was not thinking of Joe Parsons. He was thinking of Otto and Rose

Steiner. Imagining them hastily packing their bags, quickly and furtively leaving London, just as they had quickly and furtively left Hamburg all those years ago.

Steiner on the run again. Perhaps needlessly.

'What are you staring at me like that for?' asked Mr Harry Perkins truculently. 'What's the matter with me?'

'I wasn't staring at you,' replied Morgan irritably, 'I was thinking. From what you say, and other evidence, I have reason to believe that Mr Parsons and another man called on Draper at about 9.20 pm or a few minutes later, and found he was not in. Would he have called again, do you suppose?'

Perkins nodded emphatically and pulled at his bulbous nose.

'He'd called twice before, casually. On that evening he said he'd catch Draper at home, if he had to wait for him till dawn. He was proper annoyed, was Joe, that evening. But he might have called alone the second time. This other bloke, he might have got fed up with hanging around.'

'Any idea who the second man was?'

'I didn't know there was a second bloke, I'd have told you if I had, wouldn't I? Everybody here seems to think I'm a bloody fool,' remarked Perkins in a complaining tone.

Morgan said soothingly:

'No, we don't, no, we don't – you don't want to get ideas like that.'

Perkins looked mollified and settled back in his chair, waiting for the Inspector to speak.

'I suppose Parsons is not at home, is he? You're sure of that?'

'We phoned his flat several times. Then Jessie, she's one of our girls, she called there on the way to the office this morning, and found a lot of milk-bottles on the doorstep. She rang several times and got no reply. She asked the porter, but he hadn't seen him for two or three days, he said.'

'What's his address?'

The Inspector drew a scribbling-block towards him and got out his pencil. Mr Perkins said:

'Don't you know his address? I should have thought the police would have found out his address, seeing he was a friend of Bob Draper's.'

'Well, we don't know it,' said Morgan sharply, 'otherwise I wouldn't be asking for it, would I?'

'All right, all right,' replied Perkins in an injured tone. 'No need to bite my head off, is there? He lived in one of these 'ere one-room luxury flats. With a bathroom and a kitchen and –'

'Look,' said Morgan, tapping the block of paper with his silver pencil, 'would you mind just telling me the address? That's all I want.'

'Number Four Shaling Court, King's Road, Chelsea, if that's what you want. Look 'ere, Inspector, I come here of my own free will and accord – nobody forced me to, mind you – I come 'ere to do my duty as a citizen, and I don't expect you to –'

'No,' said Morgan tonelessly, 'no, I'm sorry if I was impatient Mr Perkins, but I –'

His voice died away as he picked up the telephone receiver and asked to be put through to his own room, where Shaw would be wrestling with the indignant Alice Tamworth.

'How're you doing?' he asked.

'All right,' replied Shaw guardedly.

'Listen. I want a squad car sent round at once – at once, understand? – to Number Four Shaling Court, King's Road, Chelsea. That's Joe Parsons' home address. It's a flat. They'll have to break in. I want the place searched to see if Parsons has skipped. See if his toilet things are there. Check the underclothes, suits, all the rest of it. If there's any sign that he's skipped for any length of time, warn all police forces, air ports, sea ports and –' Morgan hesitated – 'yes, and Interpol as well, to detain him for questioning in connexion with the murder of Robert George Wood, alias Draper. Of course, he may just have got browned off and gone off for a couple of days for –'

'Not just before the Derby, he wouldn't,' muttered Perkins, 'Joe wouldn't go off that way at this time of year.'

' – for a jaunt,' concluded Morgan, 'but it's unlikely.'

'Impossible,' whispered Perkins hoarsely.

'Just a minute,' Morgan turned to Perkins. 'Had he got a passport?'

' 'Course he had a passport. He used to go over to the French races.'

'He's got a passport.'

'Search warrant?' asked Sergeant Shaw perfunctorily.

'Phooey,' said Morgan.

'Description?' asked Shaw. 'Shall I go by Miss Bellamy's description?'

'Yes. Mr Perkins here confirms he was wearing a grey tweed suit and a light grey hat. When last seen, that is. I'll get a more detailed description and let you have it later. Okay?'

He replaced the receiver.

Otto Steiner had skipped, and Joe Parsons had almost certainly skipped. Otto because his nerve broke, but hottempered irascible Joe Parsons, what about him? There seemed to be only one good reason for him to run away.

For a moment he thought of Len Turner, who had run away, too, for a few hours, but he had been running away from his thoughts, or trying to. He couldn't get away from them, that was the trouble with Len. They had caught up with him and dragged him back to his little house, and then he had killed Gladys, whom he loved. He must have loved her, or he wouldn't have killed her, thought Morgan; he'd just have been indifferent, if he hadn't loved her. Now Len's thoughts would never let him go. All through the years, if he wasn't hanged – and it was unlikely that he would be – he would remain the prisoner of his thoughts.

Morgan jerked his mind back to Mr Perkins with the bulbous nose and the pimple, and dragged the scribbling block towards him.

'Now,' he said crisply, 'let's have a detailed description of Mr Joe Parsons.'

'What again? I told the other bloke what he was like.'

'Tell me, too,' said Morgan, persuasively. 'Go into as much detail as you can. We'll start right from scratch. Aged about thirty-eight – right?'

'About that,' replied Harry Perkins grudgingly.

'Height – about five feet eight inches. Right?'

Perkins nodded.

'Medium build?'

'Pretty well,' replied Perkins, 'but more stocky than not. He is a strongish bloke, on the whole.'

'Colour of hair?'

'Brown, and a bit curly. Wavy, anyway. And brown eyes. No moustache, clean shaven, he is. Fairly straight nose.'

'Has he what you might call a squarish head or a roundish one?'

Perkins considered the question for a moment, pulling at his walrus moustache, and pursing his lips.

'He's got a roundish head,' he said at length, 'and a roundish face, too. A bit red.'

Morgan thought it was no good asking about the shape of Parson's ears, or of his hands, or about his gait. Only police officers and women noticed things like that.

'What about his teeth, Mr Perkins?'

Perkins looked at Morgan with his big, sly brown eyes.

'What about 'em?' he said. 'They are his own, if that's what you mean. Just ordinary, except that one has a gold stopping in front.'

Morgan glanced down at the details. They were not particularly encouraging, because they could be applied to a thousand and one men in the country.

'Can you think of anything which might single him out? Anything special about him? Anything at all?'

Perkins shook his head.

'He is a pretty ordinary looking sort of bloke, if you ask me. His voice is a bit on the harsh side, being a bookie.'

'Does he wear a wrist-watch?'

'Now you come to mention it, he does,' said Perkins slowly. 'A gold one. Very proud of it, he is. Bought it in Italy.'

'What's it look like?'

'Square. With one of them dials you can read in the dark. He said it was dustproof and waterproof.'

'Does he wear it on a leather strap or a gold strap.'

'Gold,' said Perkins. 'Nothing but the best is good enough for Joe Parsons, as you might say.'

Inspector Morgan leaned back in his chair, chin sunk on

his chest, searching his mind for anything else that might help.

'Does he drink and smoke?'

'He likes whisky,' replied Perkins, 'so do I, come to that, but he doesn't overdo it. He'll 'ave a couple at lunch-time, and a few in the evening. Nothing much; no, he doesn't what you'd call *drink*. He smokes. Cigarettes, mostly.'

'Does he chain smoke? Are his fingers nicotine stained?'

'Not that I've noticed.'

The Inspector put down his pencil. He glanced at his wrist-watch. It was nearly twelve-thirty, and he couldn't reckon on a report from Parsons' flat for another hour or so.

He strongly suspected that Shaw would have got rid of the Tamworth woman, and gone along in the squad car. But if a police patrol-car had been in the Chelsea area, they had probably radioed it direct, in which case Shaw would have taken a Yard car and joined the uniformed men at the flat. Either way, Shaw would telephone him.

'Well, I suppose that's as far as we can get,' he said reluctantly.

'Ah,' said Perkins ponderously, 'but is it? Now 'ere's a bit that may 'elp. It may or it may not, and it's not for me to say. It's you mentioning smoking and nicotine-stained fingers that made me think of it. Mind you,' he went on, his thoughts going off at a tangent, 'the whole thing may be a mare's nest, as they say. What you might call a wild-goose chase, if I may coin a phrase, because Joe, he may be ill in hospital, for all you know.'

'Yes,' said Morgan patiently. 'Yes, he may be, but I doubt if he is. Now what were you going to say? Something about nicotine-stained fingers?'

'I was going to say – but mind you, it's only a small point, a detail like,' replied Perkins and held up a warning hand.

Morgan sighed, and looked down at the table in case Perkins should see the impatience in his eyes. You had to let people tell things their own way. It was no use hurrying them. They only became flustered or angry or both.

'Never mind, let's have it,' he said.

'It's your mention of fingers that did it,' said Perkins again.

'He has a gold signet ring, and he used to wear it on his left little finger, but now he wears it on his right little finger.'

'He does, does he?' said Morgan, trying to sound interested. He jotted the fact down on his pad. 'What made him change fingers, any idea?'

He asked the question while he was still writing, without looking up, hardly caring whether Perkins replied or not.

'He had to,' he heard Perkins say, and give a loud guffaw. 'He had to change his blooming finger, because he lost the top half of the other one! Caught it in a train door on the way to York races and had to have it cut off. So he hadn't got much finger to wear a ring on,' continued Harry Perkins, still smiling. 'That's why he changed over. Wasn't no bloody choice about it, he had to, didn't he?'

Much to Mr Perkins's annoyance, the Inspector wasn't laughing; he wasn't even smiling. He was frowning, and staring at Mr Perkins as though he thoroughly disapproved of him.

'What's up?' asked Mr Perkins, ready to become indignant again.

'You're quite sure of that?' asked Morgan. 'You're quite sure that the top part of his left little finger was missing?'

"Course I'm sure! Listen, you might imagine a bit of finger when there isn't one, but you can't imagine nothing when there's something there, can you? It don't make sense. And another thing, I was in the train when he had the accident, and there wasn't nothing imaginary about what Joe said when the porter slammed the door on his finger.'

Perkins was shaking with laughter now, his stomach wobbling, his cunning brown eyes dancing at the recollection of what was one of the high spots of his life.

Morgan sat glaring at him, his own face as immobile as though it had been hewn out of a Welsh quarry. All he wanted now was to get rid of Perkins, send him about his business and hurry back to his own room.

His heart was thumping excitedly, and his pulses would go on racing until he was back in his room, until he could lay his hands on the buff folder which contained the reports to date on the Paton street case.

He pushed his chair back, and rose to his feet.

'That'll be all for today, thank you, Mr Perkins.' He held out his hand. 'Thank you very much for calling in. If we want you again, we'll get in touch with you.'

He walked with Perkins to the entrance, slowly, pretending to listen to Mr Perkins as he rambled on about the details of the operation on Joe Parsons' little finger. About the first aid, and the hospital, and the incapacity of Joe Parsons to carry on his business for some time, and about how he, Perkins, had borne the whole responsibility upon his own shoulders.

At the doorway itself, Mr Perkins turned his face, with the bulbous nose, and pimple, the walrus moustache, and said:

'As true as I'm standing here, Joe Parsons had tears in 'is eyes when he thanked me for all I 'ad done. You'd never believe it, would you? I mean, a bloke like Joe Parsons. Tears in his eyes, that's what he had.'

Five seconds after Perkins had gone, Morgan was in the lift. A few moments later he was hurrying, half walking, half running, along the blue-grey pastel-coloured corridor to his own room.

He put his head round Shaw's door, on the way, but the Sergeant was not there. Once in his own room, he slammed the door behind him, and tore open the drawer of his desk and took out the case dossier.

Shaw came on the 'phone five minutes after Morgan had found the report he wanted. Shaw said:

'It's odd, there's nothing missing at all. Not even his razor or toothbrush. He must have lost his head and just dashed off. I take it you'll alert all the ports and police forces, all the same, sir?'

'We don't need to,' said Inspector Morgan, staring at the report of Algy Thompson, the pathologist. 'We know where Joe Parsons is, with his missing little-finger joint and his gold stopped front tooth. He's in the bloody mortuary, Fred. He's where we thought Draper was, that's where Joe Parsons is.'

Chapter 9

DRAPER was still alive, and somewhere among the fifty million people in Britain he was trying to build up a new identity, a new life.

Morgan was quite sure about that.

Draper had murdered himself, killed himself off, and in the act he had wiped out not only his own identity but the troubles which had been pressing in on him. Draper had done Draper to death, but the body he had used had been the body of Joe Parsons, the bookmaker.

He had plenty of reasons for wishing to disappear finally and forever. He had been sacked by Ted Tilling. He owed money. He had an angry and embittered wife on his track. He had the lease of a flat on his hands. He had the practical Alice Tamworth agitating for the marriage lines which he couldn't give her, and expecting the luxury and title which he had created in his imagination.

There had been Gladys Turner, and her own particular trouble, and to cap it all, not only was his blackmail money from Steiner to cease, but there was the threat that unless he began to repay all that he had received he might be faced with a prosecution and years of imprisonment. He may have laughed at the threat, as Bleaker had described, but he must have known the game was up.

So Robert George Draper, jobless, penniless, and threatened, had decided to end his own 'life'. And Joe Parsons had paid the price.

'He damned nearly succeeded,' said Morgan, eating a ham sandwich at his desk. 'He transferred his watch to Parsons' wrist, and some of his personal belongings to Parsons' pockets, he saw that the body was sufficiently burned to make it unrecognizable, and to make doubly sure, he set fire to the whole flat. If the fire brigade hadn't been on the spot so promptly, if the building had burned fiercely and partially collapsed, he'd have got away with it.'

'Makes you think,' said Shaw.

'Makes you think what?' asked Morgan, taking a mouthful of hot, strong tea.

'Makes you wonder how often people get away with murder, sir.'

Shaw had returned from Parsons's flat eager for activity, keen for orders to be sent out to search for and arrest Robert George Wood, alias Draper. But Morgan had hesitated. He knew he wasn't going to act on Shaw's suggestion, but he didn't know why, and he couldn't marshal his argument. Therefore he had said that first he was going to have something to eat. Morgan took a bite at his sandwich and said:

'It also makes you wonder how many people get wrongly convicted of murder. Look at Steiner. Motive, opportunity, everything – and to cap it all, to make things look worse, he goes and skips off.

'How would that have looked to a jury, eh? What's the good of telling a jury that he had been panicky and nervy ever since the Hitler brigade had had a bash at him? What's the good of telling 'em that? It cuts both ways, that argument. If he's that jumpy, that much unstable, he might have lost his head and killed Draper. Draper was ruining him. Draper was a threat to his son. All that sort of stuff.'

'What about the Steiners, sir?'

'What about them?'

'Well, sir – '

Shaw stopped and walked over to the window and looked out at the Embankment. He continued:

'Well, sir, after all, the poor bastard is on the run with his wife; not that I care much. As far as I'm concerned all the foreigners in England can go on the run to the ends of the earth, and I wouldn't lose any sleep. But there's a bit in the evening papers about us wanting to interview Steiner.

'He'll be reading the papers, you can reckon on that for a certainty, and he'll see it, and get the wind up even more. I thought that if we sent out a general call for the arrest of Draper, and let the Press have it, too, the Steiners would see it, and come back. Not that I care two blinking straws for the Steiners, sir,' added Shaw defensively.

Morgan shook his head. He knew his line of action now. He

also knew that Sergeant Shaw wouldn't approve, but he was prepared for that.

'How long do you think two foreigners like the Steiners, with their German accent, can stay undetected in this island, Sergeant?'

Shaw turned over the question in his mind.

'Maybe forty-eight hours, sir. Perhaps seventy-two. Not much longer.'

'And a nondescript Englishman like Draper?'

'Weeks. Maybe longer, if he's cunning and unobtrusive enough, sir.'

'Exactly,' agreed the Inspector, 'that's the answer. That's my argument. We'll pick up the Steiners soon enough, and we'll release them, of course, but quietly without fuss. No publicity. Nothing in the papers, if we can help it, and the crime boys usually play ball. Meanwhile, you can certainly put out a call for Draper's arrest, but warn all police forces not to let it leak out to the Press. Got it?

'Draper, he thinks that Otto Steiner is going to swing for this job. He thinks we don't suspect anything. He thinks he's fairly safe. He'll be careful, of course, change his appearance a bit, and all that, and he'll be hoping that one day he'll be able to slip abroad. They always hope that, not that it's ever got 'em very far. But one day one of them might manage it, and it might be Draper.'

The Inspector began to drum on the table with his fist. Softly with regular beats, while his eyes stared at his blotting pad.

'I want to get that bloody man – alive – more than I've wanted to get anybody in my life, because he's bad and vicious through and through.

'You know me, Sergeant; you know I think that most murderers aren't among the worst members of the population. You know my views. I think most of 'em kill in a moment of fright – lose their heads, kind of, or want to stun somebody, and go too far. But this bloke Draper, I want to see him in the dock. I want to see him in suspense. I want to imagine him in his cell when the Governor tells him that his reprieve has been refused. I want to think of him scared stiff when they come to fetch him.

And when nine o'clock strikes, I want to think of him disappearing through the trap, and I'll say to myself, there is one man who has deserved what he got, and I shall feel proud that I had a part in getting it for him. It's men like Draper who justify the nine-o'clock walk. The planners of murders, the blackmailers, the men who use crime as a means of easy living, and feed on others, like the grubs they are.'

Morgan stopped drumming on the table, and looked up sheepishly, and said:

'Don't take any notice, Sarge. Hate's a bad thing, and you English don't feel it so much. But I'm Welsh, and that means a mixture of Ancient Briton, Celt, and maybe a little bit of Roman, and the Romans came from Italy. Hate's bad, because it warps your judgement.'

'Yes, sir,' said Shaw and remained silent.

'Well, go on, say it,' said Morgan testily.

'Well, sir, I still think we'd do better to alert all police forces and also get it in the Press. You're cutting out the help of the public if you don't get it in the newspapers, sir. They're very observant and alert in this country.'

Morgan shook his head emphatically and fumbled in his pocket for his pipe and tobacco.

'You've forgotten one thing – money. He hasn't got much. And the opportunity to do the job cropped up the day before Tilling was to pay him off.

'He won't want to apply for work at once. That would mean coming out in the open too much. He'll be waiting to hear that Steiner has been charged with murder, or that a warrant is out for Joe Parsons. Then he'll feel even more secure. Money's his weakness at the moment.'

Morgan paused and looked Shaw in the eye, and said:

'I want a request sent out to all police forces in England. Not Scotland, Wales, or Ireland, he'd feel conspicuous there –' Morgan paused, then went on resolutely – 'I want every likely pawnshop in England checked, to see if a man answering to Draper's description has within the last couple of days pawned a gold wrist-watch and gold wrist-watch bracelet of Italian make. Square watch, waterproof, dustproof, with luminous dial. If not I want periodic checks made. Got it?'

Shaw whistled softly and stared at Morgan. Then he nodded and turned and left the room without a word. It was not for him to comment. The Inspector sat gripping his pipe tightly between his teeth.

It was his second great mistake in the Paton Street case.

Looking back on it all afterwards, the Inspector realized that he just didn't seem able to put a foot right in that case. He was destined to solve other cases later in his career, some more intricate, many demanding more concentration and longer hours, and one or two in which his Celtic intuition, which had let him down badly in the present case, proved to be of considerable value. But he freely admitted later that had his position at the Yard depended upon his handling of the Paton Street affair, he would have been reduced to the rank of a constable on the beat within a week.

At home that evening, he found himself listening, sometimes consciously, sometimes subconsciously, for the telephone to ring. He had given instructions that he was to be telephoned at any hour of the night if any development occurred. But the instrument remained silent all the evening.

He began to review the case, examining each stage, testing his actions, seeking the flaws in his handling of the investigation.

The first, and greatest, misfortune had been the mistake in identifying the body as that of Draper, but here he was inclined to absolve himself from blame. The terrible condition of the body had precluded any practical possibility of identification by anyone who knew Draper by sight. Therefore he had taken the contents of the pockets, and subsequently the inscription of the watch as establishing the corpse as that of Draper.

He blamed himself for being led astray by the cigarette end, for concentrating overmuch on Gladys Turner at the beginning, and for not instituting parallel inquiries when Tilling had mentioned that Draper owed money to Joe Parsons. On the other hand, he had been right to have James Bleaker followed; it was this action, and Bleaker's information resulting from it, which had provided the first big step forward in the case.

He was right to investigate Otto Steiner, but he was seriously at fault when he had let him go home after the last interrogation. He still felt curiously hurt about Steiner's disappearance, still felt, illogically, that in some way Steiner had broken faith, had abused the compassion which he had felt for the man.

At eleven o'clock he went to bed.

In bed he began to wonder whether, after all, he had been right to try to lure Draper into a false sense of security; whether he should not, after all, have taken Shaw's advice and instituted a nation-wide hunt, by police, by publicity in the Press and on the radio, in an endeavour to track Draper down by sheer mass hue and cry.

Long after he had put the light out, he visualized Draper, with what Tilling had called his putty-coloured complexion, sidling into some sea-port, edging up gangplanks, seeking some job on a foreign vessel which was short of crew and none too scrupulous. Some of the Greek and some of the South American-owned ships were not particular whom they took on in an emergency. In any case, they would have no reason to suspect Draper, because there was no publicity about him. As far as Draper was concerned, there was a complete news blackout, and he, Chief Detective Inspector Morgan of Scotland Yard, by his own wish and orders, was the cause of it.

To him would be the credit if his gamble succeeded; and on his shoulders, and his alone, would fall the blame if the man made a get-away.

He fell asleep thinking more of blame than of credit, and knew that was at least one reason, though not the most important, why he hated Draper so much. Draper had made his self-confidence falter.

Throughout the night the telephone by his bedside remained quiet.

*

For any demon spirit with a sense of fun, a very nice situation indeed was now brewing up. It would not be stretching the imagination too far to picture such a spirit flitting among other kindred spirits, telling them to gather round to watch forthcoming events, because something pretty laughable was about to occur.

Hitherto, there hadn't been anything particularly ripe, even though there had been incidents which were not devoid of amusement.

Good old Len, for instance, had played his part manfully, and the way he had all along insisted on sticking his neck into the noose, possibly literally, had certainly whiled away an hour or two in the great Eternity of time.

Gladys too had been good sport, while she lasted, and especially when she had used that stupid phrase about Draper giving her something which Len couldn't, and had been killed for it. The episode had been enlivening, admittedly, but not outstanding, because down below that sort of imbecility was always happening.

But now something rich and rare was in the offing, and it was certainly worthwhile watching Chief Detective Inspector Morgan as he swayed in a No. 11 bus along King's Road, Chelsea, and then swayed in an Underground train from Sloane Square to Westminster, and finally walked to his office by the Thames.

A number of people wrote to the Inspector from time to time. Old lags out of prison asked his help, elderly ladies sought his advice, young men queried points about conditions in the police force, and so forth. He was a man who had had much publicity in his time, and a heavy postbag was the price he paid for it.

He put his letters aside on arrival at the Yard, because out of the town of Winchester, in the county of Hampshire, had come surprisingly good news which raised his spirits to the peak.

It was a telephoned message from the Winchester police, and it stated, briefly and without frills, that a man undoubtedly answering to the description of Robert George Draper had pawned a gold watch of Italian make not twenty-four hours ago. Furthermore, the man had seemed nervous and anxious to get out of the shop. But when the pawnbroker, who, like all pawnbrokers, was always on the look-out for stolen goods, had commented on the fact that he seemed to be in a hurry, the man had said that he was not in a hurry, he was merely nervous and embarrassed because he had never pawned anything in his life before.

The reply had seemed so frank and natural that the pawnbroker's suspicions had been lulled. Nevertheless, he had made a note of the matter, intending to mention it to one of the detectives who periodically called at his shop and examined his goods.

Winchester police were now engaged in visiting all hotels and lodging-houses in the city and its vicinity, and road patrols had been instructed to keep a look-out.

To Shaw, who had brought the message in, Morgan said:

'He may be making for Southampton, or again he may double on his tracks and make for somewhere like Liverpool. But he's a Southerner and probably feels more at home in the south, so we'd better tip off Southampton.'

'Do you think he'll travel by night, sir?'

'I doubt it,' said Morgan, 'I doubt it very much. He's not on the run, remember, not yet. He still doesn't know that we know he is alive. Apart from not attracting too much attention, I doubt if he's taking much trouble to hide. That was the whole point of not announcing publicly that we want him; that was part of my plan, if you remember?'

There was a faint undertone of pride in the Inspector's voice; almost imperceptible, but present none the less. It was excusable. The gamble was succeeding, and he felt he was getting his old touch back.

He was in very good spirits indeed, was Inspector Morgan, which made the subsequent developments all the more trying for him.

It stemmed from the fact that Morgan did not know his Germans, and neither did Shaw for that matter, and there was no reason why they should have done.

It is true that Otto Steiner was a Jew, but it is also true that his family had lived in the German fatherland for several generations. They had, one may assume, imbibed from the water, soil, and air, from the pine woods, and from their fellow citizens, certain national traditions and customs, certain virtues and vices, which must have been more or less in constant conflict with other atavistic instincts inherited from their Middle Eastern ancestors.

The Jewish people, at the darkest moments in their history, have shown a tenacity, a tough resilience, an instinct for survival at any cost, which is in marked contrast to a neurotic tendency among individual Aryan Germans to collapse in despair when things are going badly.

The situation which faced Morgan soon after he arrived at the Yard was due to the fact that at the time when he had need of Jewish resilience, Otto Steiner's Germanic streak had supervened.

'Any trace of the Steiners, Sergeant?' Morgan asked casually.

'I was coming to that, sir. The girl's downstairs waiting to see you.'

'Rachel Steiner? What about?'

Shaw glanced down at the slip of paper in his hand which visitors have to fill in, stating whom they wish to see and why.

'She's written, "About my parents", sir.'

Morgan thought for a moment, and said:

'Better see what she wants. She probably wants to know if we've any news. Hop downstairs and see her, will you?'

'As a matter of fact, I've seen her, sir,' replied Shaw, his eyes fixed on Morgan's face.

'What's up? Why are you looking at me like that?' asked the Inspector suddenly.

'Well, sir,' said Shaw, still staring at the Inspector, 'I'm afraid there's been a bit of bad luck, one way and another. From what she said, I gathered that Mr and Mrs Steiner were dead, sir.'

The Inspector said nothing for a few seconds.

He heard his heart pounding, and felt the red blood, signal of shock and emotion, creep slowly up his neck to the lower part of his face, then up his face itself, over his forehead, and into his hair, so that the scalp tingled and the whole face and head burned.

He knew perfectly well what Sergeant Shaw was thinking, because he was thinking the same as the Sergeant. He was thinking that if the true facts had been published in time, Steiner would have known he was cleared. That's what the Sergeant was thinking.

He was thinking that if his superior officer had been sensible, if he had taken the straightforward normal course, instead of making some crack-pot attempt to be clever and subtle, tubby Otto Steiner and his fat wife would have been alive at that moment.

That's what the Sergeant was thinking.

He was thinking that when you've had a good many years at the police game, and when you've had a lot of success, you become obstinate, you won't listen to the advice of your subordinates, you think you always know best. Then this sort of thing happened.

That's what the Sergeant was thinking.

He saw Shaw swallow. The Sergeant said:

'I gathered from the girl, sir, that there's probably a letter for you. Shall I have a look?'

Shaw leaned forward and picked up the mail on Morgan's desk, and began to go through it, slowly and methodically, placing the typed letters tidily in a heap on the desk, scrutinizing carefully the handwritten ones.

'This looks like it, sir.'

The Inspector stretched out his hand and took the letter and looked at the handwriting, and then turned the envelope over. Germanic, methodical, punctilious to the end, Steiner had carefully written on the back: From O. Steiner, Alexander Hotel, Buxton, Derbyshire.

Morgan opened it. Apart from having written his name wrong, the letter was well spelt, the grammar and phrasing very nearly correct, the handwriting old-fashioned but firm. Except for the postscript, the letter was logical and unemotional:

Dear Inspector Morgon,

This letter is tell you that I quite understand the difficulties of the police detectives who are trying to find out the murderer of Mr Draper. Also I wish to say that I am sorry that I left London without telling you, but in the then circumstances I found it difficult to think with clearness, because things were going round so much in my head.

I have now been able to think with clearness, and I think there is only one thing which is sensible to do. I did not kill Mr Draper, but I know that there is much evidence against me. If I could have said guilty, at a trial, and no evidence, I think I would have done so, but you said no. Also there is the inquest. Mr Bleaker is not a bad man, and Miss Brueckmann is an old friend, so now there is only you and the officer with the red hair who might tell somebody about Julius which I ask you from my heart not to do. He is a good boy. My daughter Rachel is a good girl. I cannot do any more for them, and now they must drown or swim alone.

I have tried to tell myself that Mr Draper and all people who do wrong are not bad men but sick in the mind, but I am sorry, I must think even at this moment that Mr Draper was a wicked man, although I hope that God will not condemn him for always. I hope that I too will be forgiven sometime for what I do now. Perhaps one day there will not be communists and Fascists and then such troubles will not arise.

My wife does not know, and thinks I have come here suddenly for a rest, because I could not stand it any longer, which is in a way. I said I had told you I was coming here. We have fought many things together, and it is better that she is not left alone. She is asleep now, and I think she looks very happy and handsome, and I have kissed her goodnight.

I wish to state that I have no complaint against you or the other detective. I have lived a good many years, and have had much more happiness than sadness, I think. God has been very merciful to me. It is after lunch. I shall now take some sleeping tablets, which I have been taking since the Hamburg time, and in this way I shall not smell the gas. First, I shall take this letter downstairs.

Yours faithfully
O. Steiner

P.S. Please help Rachel. I came here so she would not find us. It would have been a shock. I am not afraid. How should there be day without night, or an awakening without sleep? I am tired of fighting. I go to meet death like a lover his mistress. Somebody said that, I think.

The Inspector stared at the old-fashioned writing. He tossed the letter across to Shaw, and got up and walked quickly to the window, and tried to make out the traffic going along the Embankment.

The buses, the red London buses, and the private cars, and they with their colours so gay in the sun, and the sunshine itself so clean after the rain, and shining down out of all the glory of the radiant blue sky.

After a minute or two he heard the slight sound as Shaw moved and replaced the letter on the desk.

'He registered in a false name,' muttered Shaw. 'He must have done.'

'You'd better show her up here,' said Morgan, without turning round.

'Yes, sir. Actually, she's got some young chap with her.'

'Show them both up, if she wants to bring him, too.'

He heard the door close as the Sergeant left the room. But he did not move from the window. He remained staring out across the river, at the buildings on the South Bank of the Thames, reviewing again the errors he had made in the Paton Street Case and how the mistakes had occurred. In those few moments he suddenly felt stifled by the Metropolis, contaminated by the slime and the dirt and the intrigue of the cases he had handled during his long career.

The sense of mission which he had brought to London, the gay cloak of adventure which he had donned when he took the train in Wales as a young man, the eagerness to test his wits, the zest for work, all this had inevitably been dimmed or sullied by the years. But something had remained, and that was the confidence in his own integrity. Now he felt even that was in jeopardy.

Had he sent a police car to pick up Steiner on the night he had conducted the last interrogation, Steiner would have been alive. Vanity, a reluctance to show that he had made a mistake in not detaining the man, had stopped him from doing so. A wish to show himself to be the great detective with a remarkable flair had stopped his ears to Shaw's advice about publicity. And lurking in the background of his mind was the realization that he had wanted to delay as long as possible – until an arrest had been made, in fact – the revelation that the police, and himself as the man in charge, had been hoodwinked into identifying the body as that of Draper.

During the minutes when Shaw was out of the room, Chief Detective Inspector Morgan's resignation from the Metropolitan Police Force was balanced on a knife-edge.

Then he heard the door open, and swung round, chin on chest, bulky and determined, and the deciding factor in his attitude was the emotion which he had so deprecated to Shaw – hatred.

Hatred of Robert George Wood, alias Draper, who had now been primarily responsible for the deaths of four people, Parsons, Gladys Turner, and the Steiners; whose wickedness, in addition, had led to the incarceration of the man Turner on a capital charge of killing his wife.

He had expected to meet a tearful and distraught woman, and he saw at once that he had been wrong. She was alone, very pale, but perfectly composed, as she took the chair which the Inspector offered her.

Looking at her, Morgan wondered whether either of her parents had resembled her in appearance when they had been young, or whether Rachel Steiner had inherited her looks from some grandparent.

She was only of medium height, but of slender build, the head small, the hair very dark and wavy. He guessed that her complexion, even normally, was ivory pale, but the lips were full and red, the mouth sensitive, and her nose had a delicate straightness which recalled pictures he had seen of the royal houses of the Pharoahs.

Her eyes were grey and calm, and although she wore spectacles, she had taken care to ensure that they should be an adornment rather than otherwise. The frame which held the lenses was pointed at the outer sides, and up-tilted, blue in colour to tone with the navy blue of her linen suit, and it lent a piquancy to her oval face. Under the jacket of her suit she wore a white silk blouse, and at her throat was a round brooch of gold and small turquoise stones.

When she spoke her voice was even and controlled, and carried a trace of an American accent, a reminder of the war years she had passed in the United States.

'I guess I just called to congratulate you, Inspector,' she said. 'I guess you've succeeded where the Nazis failed. He didn't die from gas poisoning in Auschwitz, he died from gas poisoning in democratic England, and by his own hand. That's something Hitler couldn't make him do. I reckon you must be pretty proud of yourself, and your interrogations, Inspector.'

For the second time within the space of a few minutes, the Inspector flushed scarlet. Anger at the injustice of her words, a sense of grievance because his feelings of compassion for Otto Steiner had led to the man's death, combined to send the blood once again to his face.

Shaw was different. Shaw just regarded it, in his own words, as a 'bit of bad luck'. Shaw wasn't going to have any foreigner, naturalized or not, being rude to a Chief Detective Inspector, whatever the circumstances. Shaw looked quickly at Morgan, and then said:

'There's no need to adopt that tone, madam; no need at all. The Inspector, here, was very considerate to your father. Mr Steiner could have had worse treatment by a long chalk than he had from the Inspector and me.'

When she did not reply, did not even turn her head or give any indication that she had heard, he added:

'There was a lot of evidence against your father, madam, and it's no good saying there wasn't. He wasn't as frank as he might have been, and it's no good saying otherwise.'

'Am I to understand that you still think he was guilty of the murder of this Mr Draper?'

She addressed her question to Morgan, looking at him coldly, her hands folded in her lap.

'No,' replied Morgan after a pause. 'No, you can take it that his name has been cleared.'

'Thank you. It's a little late, of course, but thank you for the information.'

Morgan was trying to make up his mind whether to tell her the truth about Draper and Parsons, weighing the pros and cons, debating how much she could be trusted to be discreet. He heard Shaw say:

'If he hadn't run away, madam, this would never have happened. And it wouldn't have happened if he had been arrested. Only the Inspector was sorry for him, he wanted to give him the benefit of the doubt until he was certain about him.'

Shaw was sometimes surprisingly perspicacious.

'Miss Steiner –'

'Doctor Steiner, if you wish to be accurate.'

'I beg your pardon – Doctor Steiner. Did your father write to you as well as to me?'

'He did.'

'Did he explain about Draper and your brother?'

'I knew about Julius, of course, but I didn't know about Draper. Not till I got his last – '

The twitching of the muscles around the full, red lips. The trembling of the lips themselves; and the hands in the lap, the fingers interlaced, gripping each other more tightly. Movement in the column of the throat, and the head not held so high. The gaze of the eyes dropping to the line of the desk in front of her, the head sinking lower, and a slight shudder of the shoulders, and then others more pronounced, and a gasp as the first sob burst through the chains of her self-control.

Shaw, embarrassed, looked down at the floor.

But Morgan, Welsh sympathy aflame, heaved himself to his feet and pushed his way round his desk, and laid his hand on Rachel Steiner's shoulder.

Once, between the sobs and the convulsive shuddering, he heard her cry, 'Poor Daddy!', and the Inspector murmured: 'He's at peace, now, see?' and reproached himself for the trite inadequacy of his words.

His voice seemed to remind her of the pressure of his hand on her shoulder. She took one hand for a moment from her face, and snatched at the Inspector's hand, and flung it from her, and jerked her head up, staring at him with tear-drowned eyes through misty spectacles. Controlling herself for a moment she flung her dislike at him in a jerky spate of words.

'You killed him! You can say what you like, but you killed him with your cruel questioning and bullying. Daddy would never hurt anybody; but you've killed him, killed him and Mummy; you killed them both! You succeeded where Hitler failed! You're as bad as Draper; Draper didn't kill him, he only took his money, but you've taken his life, and now they're dead, Daddy and Mummy are dead, and you did it, and it's your fault! It's all your fault, your fault!'

Quite an outburst for a girl devoted to the cold study of medical science.

*

At three o'clock in the afternoon Morgan received a report which raised his hopes.

Shaw, on his instructions, had arranged with the Buxton police that the true identities of the Steiners should be withheld from publication for forty-eight hours.

Meanwhile, his own hatred of Draper was becoming almost pathological and everything else was subordinated to it. He had even decided against telling Rachel Steiner the true identity of the dead man; and the girl, under pressure from Shaw, had agreed to keep temporarily from the Press the news of her parents' death. Stubbornly, in the teeth of tragedy, Morgan decided to persist in his original plan of allowing Draper no inkling of the fact that he was being sought by the police forces of the entire country. He knew that Shaw disapproved, but he no longer cared.

Now came the report that a man dressed in the manner described by the Winchester pawnbroker, a stranger in the town, had been traced to a small hotel in Winchester, where he had spent the night, and left that morning for an unknown destination. He had filled in the hotel register in the name of R. Brown, of 19, Pendale Drive, Wimbledon.

Shaw, checking in the current Post Office Street Directory, stated that no such road existed in Wimbledon, and a further check with the Wimbledon police showed that no road had been so named in recent months.

A check among Winchester taxi-drivers produced a driver who stated that he had driven such a man from the hotel to the station, where he had seen the man hand his suitcase to a porter and heard him say that he wished to catch the Southampton train, on his way to Havant. For a man wishing to infiltrate quietly into Southampton, Havant seemed as good a place as any to make for.

By six o'clock in the evening, while Morgan's hopes were still high, a search of Havant and district turned up a Mr P. Prendergast, a commercial traveller, who admitted under some pressure, and in a sheepish fashion, that he was the so-called R. Brown of 19, Pendale Drive, Wimbledon. He had recently inherited some property from a brother, and among the property was a gold wrist-watch, and since his lady friend had moved to Winchester, and he was temporarily embarrassed for a little ready money, he had pawned the watch. He was assured that Mrs Prendergast would not be informed of the incident, and the opportunity was taken to stress the obligation of all travellers to fill in hotel registers truthfully. No action would be taken in this case, in spite of the trouble and expense to which he had put the Hampshire police.

Other reports from different parts of the country were now coming in by teleprinter and by telephone. Lancashire produced an alarm, when the Bolton police reported that a man answering to Draper's description had knocked down a police officer who had stopped him to question him and made off. Recaptured an hour later, the man had turned out to be a confidence trickster who had just pulled a fast one on a jeweller in the town. He was now detained.

Cheshire sent a flash that they might have found the wanted man, and then hurriedly cancelled it fifteen minutes later, offering no explanation.

One quite hopeful report came from nearby Sussex, where a vigilant police patrol car wirelessed that it was in pursuit of a grey Austin saloon reported stolen from Redhill during the night, and now being driven by a man who might be Draper. The chase proved short and ludicrous, the driver proving to be the legal owner of the car, who had not yet troubled to inform the police that he had retrieved the car from his brother, who had taken it from the garage, unknown to him, during his absence from the house.

Night fell, and Inspector Morgan's spirits fell with it.

Twenty-four hours later, there was still no firm indication that Draper had been found, or even seen. Morgan, convinced as ever that lack of money would bring him into the open, toyed with the idea of trying to have the announcement of the Steiners' deaths withheld for a period beyond the agreed forty-eight hours. He thought of pleading with Rachel Steiner, with the Derbyshire police, even with the Press by means of a circulated appeal to all editors of national newspapers and to all editors of newspapers in Derbyshire.

But he abandoned the idea. The practical difficulties were too great. In all honesty, he could not hazard even a guess when Draper's funds might be exhausted. Possibly they were already exhausted, but possibly he had enough to last him weeks. Maybe he even had enough to bribe his way aboard some ship sailing to South America.

It was this latter consideration which weighed most with Morgan. He decided that if the man was not arrested within the agreed time, he would also set Interpol humming, alerting the police of the world to watch for Robert George Wood, alias Robert George Draper, aged thirty-eight, height five feet eight inches, brown hair, brown eyes, oval face, putty-coloured complexion, wanted for the murder of Joseph Parsons, at 127, Paton Street, London, on the night of June 5th. If Draper intended to flee the country, or if he had somehow succeeded in fleeing already, the sooner that was done the better.

The Inspector had only one other hope, and that was a slender one indeed.

Chapter 10

WITH a feeling of numb disappointment, Rachel Steiner watched the last of the passengers disperse at the London air terminal. Julius, who should have been among them, was not there.

At first she thought he might still be in the coach which had brought the passengers from the air-port. Perhaps a piece of luggage was missing. A wallet, maybe. Or he had met an acquaintance and been detained, listening impatiently to a stream of gossip, while all the time he was wanting to tear himself away and go to the sister he knew to be waiting for him. Julius was always over-courteous.

But he did not come. She stood alone, feeling the warm tears gather in her eyes, at a loss what to do. Dr George Stafford was the only person in the world who meant anything to her now. And George Stafford had tactfully assumed that she would wish to be alone with her brother during the first evening. He had gone out of town.

Had she known the name of the people with whom he was

staying, she might have telephoned him, believing that there are times in life when one is so unhappy that one can be deliberately selfish. She knew he would have made some excuse, said perhaps that he had to return to the hospital, and that he would have come back to London to her. But she could not recall the name.

She was going to marry him, she knew that. Ever since the time when she had learned that her parents had left London, he had been steadfastly at her side. Had she proved to be the daughter of a murderer, had the blaze of notoriety descended upon her, it would, she knew, only have increased his devotion. He was that kind of man.

She glanced at the clock, and saw it was nine-thirty. She had had nothing to eat, imagining that she might have supper with Julius on his arrival. So now, although she was not hungry, she went to a buffet and forced herself to eat a sandwich and drink a cup of coffee.

She made a detour on the way back to Hampstead, calling in at the hospital on the pretext of inquiring about the state of a patient in whom she was particularly interested. In reality, she was seeking human company, somebody to talk to, something to distract her mind from the burdens of responsibility which were pressing on her.

Julius, when he arrived, would not be able to stay more than two or three days. There would be the house to dispose of, the question of whether to restock the shop and instal a manager or sell it. Above all, the problem of telling such a story to Julius as would conceal from him, at any rate for the time being, the fact that his father had been blackmailed as a result of his youthful activities. That was something, she decided, which might be revealed after the passage of years. For the moment, the tragedy of his parents' death would be enough for Julius to bear, without the burden of feeling in some way responsible for the circumstances which led up to it.

She took an Underground train to Hampstead, and arrived home just before eleven o'clock. All the way from the Underground station to Risburgh Road she had been steeling herself for the moment when she must return to the familiar surroundings of her home, be brought face to face with the furniture and little personal objects which were so closely associated with her parents. It was one reason why she was so desperately disappointed at her brother's failure to arrive. She would, at least, have had an opportunity to bustle about preparing his bed and setting his room in order, and this in itself would have left her less time to grieve.

Suddenly it occurred to her that he might have taken an earlier plane, been unable to send a cable in time, and that he might be at home now, waiting for her. She quickened her step as she turned into Risburgh Road, convinced of the correctness of her supposition, certain that she would find the lights on in the drawing-room, a suitcase in the hall.

But the house was in darkness. The curtains were drawn. An early moon cast its light on the small bay windows. For a moment she hesitated, tempted to return to the hospital, to spend the night, as she had the previous one, in the staff room. But there had to be a return some time. She told herself that she could not postpone it indefinitely.

She let herself in, switched on the hall light, and at once noticed the cable lying on the floor below the letter slot in the door. It read:

UNAVOIDABLY DELAYED, ARRIVING AIR TERMINAL 6 P.M. TOMORROW FRIDAY. LOVE JULIUS.

She put the cable on the hall table, and went through the house, switching on the lights in all the rooms. At first, she could not have said exactly why she did this. She was not superstitious, did not fear darkness and supernatural visitations. But after a while as she went into each room, and switched on the lights, and stared around, she realized that in effect she was forcing herself to get the worst over at once.

She was staring at things and not only repressing her emotions, but barring all associations from her mind. She found herself looking at some underclothes, a needle, some reels of silk, and for a moment imagined her mother mending the underclothes when her father had returned that last night, and said in his sudden nervy way that he needed a change, that he must go away, that he couldn't stand it any longer, that they must go that same night.

169

She clenched her fists and drove the thoughts from her and said to herself: underclothes, a needle, reels of silk – inanimate objects, neither feeling nor radiating emotions, neither joy, nor sadness.

In her parents' bedroom there were some shoes by a chest-of-drawers, a dress over the back of a chair, a photograph of a wedding group, and on the mantelpiece an old fountain pen which had belonged to her father. She looked at each object in turn, slowly and deliberately, saying to herself: footwear fashioned from leather, cloth woven from wool, an impression caused by light falling upon paper treated with sensitized emulsion, a vulcanite container and a metal nib. All manufactured for commercial reasons, partly used, and comparatively valueless.

She remembered that the pen no longer worked, that a man in a stationer's shop had said that the rubber bag was perished, that it was a cheap pen, not worth repairing.

She walked to the mantelpiece, deliberately and unhurriedly, and picked up the pen, and crossed the room and flung it into the waste-paper basket which stood by her mother's dressing-table.

'Junk,' she said aloud, infusing a tone of contempt into her voice. 'The house is full of junk. I can't imagine why people keep so much junk.'

She went downstairs, and into the drawing-room, and switched on the radio, and twiddled the knob until she found an American station broadcasting from Germany. She tuned in and turned the volume controller on to 'Loud', and went into the kitchen and slammed a saucepan on to the electric stove and warmed some milk.

'You're my kitten, and I guess I'm bitten, through and through by you,' announced an American singer in a voice which filled the house. She thought for a moment about the neighbours and what they would be saying, and did not care.

She sat in the kitchen, drinking the milk, smoking a final cigarette, carefully studying some notes in her case-book. It was a remarkable performance for a sensitive and imaginative girl.

When she had finished, she washed up the cup and saucer

and the saucepan, and went upstairs to her bedroom. Chief Detective Inspector Morgan calculated later that the time must have been about ten minutes to one on the morning of June 8th.

✳

There was a little brass gong in the hall passage-way. It stood on a narrow table, between the dining-room and the kitchen. It was a flimsy little affair, consisting of two metal upright pieces, a crosspiece from which the round gong was suspended by string, and a crosspiece lower down, with two metal extensions, upon which the hammer rested.

It was the sound of the little brass gong crashing to the floor which woke Dr Rachel Steiner from her sleep.

At first she thought it might have been part of a dream, but as far as she could remember she had not been dreaming. Then she thought for a second or two that it might have been her imagination, and turned over on her other side to try to get to sleep again.

But she knew it was not imagination. She knew that in fact the brass gong had fallen down, and she knew that that was why her body was so tense and rigid.

She took a deep breath, exhaled, and deliberately made herself relax her limbs. Okay, the brass gong had fallen down – so what? Why shouldn't the brass gong fall down? Pictures fell from walls from time to time, and if the string attaching the gong to the frame had finally parted, why shouldn't the brass gong fall down? What, in fact, was to prevent the gong from falling to the floor? String didn't last for ever, did it? No, it didn't. And what's more, she couldn't ever remember that piece of string breaking and being renewed. Well, it had obviously broken now, and that's why the brass gong had fallen to the floor, and that was what she had heard, and that was what had woken her up, and that was that.

A little brass gong couldn't hurt anybody when it fell to the ground. It was an inanimate object, made for commerce. Like the shoes, and the woollen dress, and the photograph, and the old fountain pen. There were no such things as ghosts,

171

and the supernatural was a lot of bunk, though poltergeists were difficult to explain.

She found to her annoyance that after about half a minute she had gone all stiff and tense again, and that she was straining her ears for any further sounds in the house.

This time she did not tell herself to relax. Instead, she went on listening, but after about two minutes, during which the only sound was that of a cat screaming in a nearby garden, she snuggled down further into the bed and closed her eyes.

A clock in the hall struck the hour of two. The house was quiet again. The cat was quiet, too. In the distance an aeroplane droned through the night, high up in the sky. In an hour or two Julius would be in the air. In seven hours, she would be seeing George Stafford again at the hospital.

Better still, in two or three hours it would be daylight.

Two or three hours was not long.

Two or three hours was one hundred and twenty minutes or one hundred and eighty minutes. It didn't sound long, put that way. What's more, there might be a little lightening of the sky in less time than that. The moonlight was all right, but it wasn't the same as daylight. It was the last time she would be sleeping in the house alone. She wouldn't stay there when Julius went back to America.

It was not that she was nervous about sleeping there alone; no, certainly not, because to a logical mind trained in the science of medicine there was nothing to be afraid of. That was obvious. She wouldn't tell George how scared she had been when the string holding the little brass gong broke, and the gong fell to the floor. Nor had she been scared – not really. Merely tense, alert, you might say – a state of automatic nerve reaction acquired during the gruelling process of evolution, of the survival of the fittest, and no more to be controlled than the instinct to raise one's hand to ward off a blow.

Still, she would move into digs somewhere when Julius went back. She would not sleep alone in the house again. It was the last night. Two to three hours and it would be daylight, and the last night would be over.

Strange to think of it as the last night.

Suddenly, her heart gave a great jump and began to race.

She found difficulty in breathing, because the little brass gong was one thing, but the loose stair-rod was another.

She knew the stair-rod. It was the fourth rod from the top. Her mother had been intending to do something about it for some time. Her father said it was dangerous. Somebody might break their neck.

There was no string on the stair-rod which could break suddenly. There was only one thing which could disarrange the stair-rod so that one end clattered on the boards at the side of the carpet.

Rachel Steiner sat up on one elbow, trying to make herself breathe normally, think clearly, take some kind of action, anything. There was no bedside telephone extension. Now it seemed that the intruder, having already made so much noise and apparently woken nobody, was feeling more sure of himself.

She heard the creak of a board on the landing, once, and then again, and then an indeterminate kind of scrabbling noise and then a faint click as the door handle of the room formerly occupied by her parents was turned.

Rachel Steiner panicked in the sense that she was torn between an instinct to scream for help, or to pretend to be asleep; she had some wild recollection of somebody saying that burglars did not become violent unless they were disturbed. In the event, she did nothing.

She lay, terror-stricken, supporting her weight on her right elbow and arm, her heart thumping so terribly that she could hardly breathe, her face screwed up in fear, the back of her left hand pressed against her mouth.

The noise of her own heart-beats prevented her from hearing what was going on outside her room, and it was not until she saw, in the moonlight, the black line between the door and the lintel grow thicker and then gradually, almost imperceptibly wider, that she knew for a certainty that somebody was coming into the room with extreme caution, opening the door inch by inch, stopping once, for a full fifteen seconds, when the door gave a slight creak, and then persevering with the slow opening.

Rachel Steiner wanted to scream now. But she couldn't.

Her voice passage seemed to be choked by pounding blood and even her brain refused to function, for she found herself feverishly and absurdly searching for the right words or noise to make. At last, by a great effort, she managed to control her breathing sufficiently to emit a noise which was between a groan and a gasp, a pitiful, smothered sound such as is made by a sleeper in the grip of a nightmare. Then she managed to speak. In a voice which was half whimper, half whisper, she said:

'Who is that? Who are you? What do you want?'

Almost at once a hand appeared and switched on the bedroom light.

It has to be remembered that Rachel Steiner knew Robert Draper, in the sense that she had seen him several times and had spoken briefly to him once or twice, but that since Morgan had not confided in her, she knew Draper to have been murdered and his body partially consumed by flames.

So when he came noiselessly into the room, it was not surprising that she dropped back on to her pillow in a dead faint.

He was sitting on the side of her bed when she recovered consciousness, holding a cup of water in his left hand. He had taken his pocket handkerchief and dipped it into the water, and was dabbing her face and murmuring reassuring words in a curiously soothing voice.

'I am so sorry, so very sorry, Dr Steiner,' he murmured apologetically. 'I do realize – believe me, I do realize – that it has been a terrible shock to you, a dreadful, dreadful shock. Do believe me when I say that only the most urgent necessity – a necessity which is far more your concern than mine – has compelled me to call on you in this frightening fashion. But there, we will talk about that in a minute. For the moment you must relax.'

When she continued to stare at him without speaking, he began to admonish her, his soft brown eyes smiling down at her out of his putty-coloured face.

'There, now, close your eyes for a few moments and try to breathe more regularly. That's better. Look, I am going to lay this wet handkerchief along your forehead for a minute or two.'

When he had done so, he began to stroke her bare forearm

with his soft, pudgy hand, and although his touch was repugnant to her she did not protest or withdraw her arm, because she felt instinctively that there was no sensuality behind his actions. He was genuinely trying to soothe her, and when he had stroked her arm for a few seconds, he finished by giving it a fatherly little pat, and got up and went and sat in a chair by the grate. A moment later, he had jumped up and crossed the room and pulled the curtains.

'We don't want the neighbours to get wrong ideas, do we? After all, in your profession, one has to be careful, is that not so?'

He smiled at her knowingly, archly, his manner that of a firm but benevolent maiden aunt towards a niece of very tender years.

Rachel Steiner said nothing. She had a brain which normally was cool and analytical. The fatigue and strain of the previous thirty-six hours, the loneliness of the house and the darkness, had momentarily thrown her off balance. But now she was almost recovered. She was suffering from reaction, which showed itself in occasional bursts of trembling, but these grew less frequent and finally ceased.

As she lay with her eyes closed, the wet handkerchief across her forehead, she was trying to make sense out of the fact that Draper, whom she had believed murdered, whom at one time her father had been suspected of killing, was very much alive and visiting the house secretly at night.

But if Draper was alive, then somebody else had been killed. Who had killed that somebody else? Her father had gone to his death still believing that Draper was the victim, even understanding in his logical German way that the police should have built up a case against himself. He had written as much in his last letter. Her father was fundamentally a religious man. On the brink of eternity he would tell the truth as he knew it.

Why had Draper disappeared? Why had he allowed the whole country to believe that he was the victim? Why had he come to the house now, furtively, in the small hours?

She did not know the answer to the last question, but she guessed the answer to the first two, and shuddered.

'Cold?' asked Draper solicitously. 'Perhaps you have a bed-wrap, a dressing-gown. May I get it for you? These June nights can be chilly in the early hours.'

She sat up in bed, and groped for her spectacles on the side table, and put them on. She could see him more clearly now. Dressed in a grey suit, and on top of it a light fawn overcoat. White shirt, semi-stiff white collar, navy blue tie with white dots. Brown brogue shoes, neat and well cleaned. Brown hat and gloves by the side of his chair. Trousers well pressed. A general air of modest prosperity.

'I don't get it,' she said in a frightened voice. 'I just don't get it. They said you were dead, they said – '

'I know, I know,' said Draper regretfully. 'A mistake was made, and as you see, I'm very much alive.'

He smiled playfully, like a conjuror producing a rabbit from a hat.

'I still don't get what it's all about. And how did you get in? And what the hell do you mean by coming in here at this hour of the night? I've a darned good mind to kick you out right away.'

Best to adopt an indignant air. Best to act naturally. He was watching her closely as she spoke, sitting very still, his brown eyes unblinking but the pupils moving very slightly, up and down, as he scanned her face.

'I just want a talk,' he replied evenly. 'Five minutes. Ten minutes. That's all. Not more. In your own interests, see? Just a private talk.'

'I guess my interests could have waited till morning, I – '

He interrupted her quickly:

'No! No, they couldn't! Believe me, they couldn't. I got in through the kitchen window, at the back by the lane.'

He went on confidentially. 'Do you know I once knew a burglar, who told me that if you examine a house carefully you can nearly always find some window that has not been closed properly. Interesting, is it not? You wouldn't think people would be so careless, would you? They go to all the trouble of locking and bolting their doors, and then they leave a window not properly secured. Strange really.'

He seemed genuinely puzzled by the vagaries of human

nature. Rachel Steiner took the handkerchief off her forehead and sat up.

'I'd like to know why you didn't come to the front door, at a civilized time, that's what I'd like to know.'

She asked herself again, if Draper wasn't murdered, who was? Draper was the killer, and Draper was on the run, that seemed clear. Hence the stealth, the nocturnal visit. She heard him say:

'I know, I know – it has been most alarming for you. Most shocking experience. I apologize. But now let me –'

'I reckon this is a lot of hooey. I just don't see what you're getting at. You let yourself be thought dead, and suddenly you turn up at –'

'I will explain. It's very simple, and yet very important. I –'

'Okay, okay,' she interrupted irritably. She was in full control of herself now. 'If you insist on talking, I can't stop you. If you'll get out of my bedroom, and go downstairs to the drawing-room, I'll put a house-coat on and come down.'

She saw the pupils of his eyes flick to the side-table by her bed, and knew he was looking to see if she had a telephone in the room. His face brightened.

'And a cup of tea, perhaps? What about a nice cup of tea? I think that would do you good. Look, you just put your house-coat on, and your bedroom slippers,' he said, in his fussy, mothering way, 'and I'll pop down and put the kettle on. Right?'

Before she could answer, he had got up and left the room. She noticed that he had an unusually light, quick step, and a way of moving which indicated that he knew exactly what he was going to do, and how.

When she went downstairs he was bustling about in the kitchen, peering into tins to find where the tea was kept, getting the milk out of the refrigerator, clattering with cups and saucers. But when he had heard her coming downstairs he put his head round the kitchen door.

'Hello,' he had said cheerfully, his eyes looking beyond her, calculating the distance to the front door, and she knew that if she had tried to run for it he would have been at her long before she could turn the key in the lock and draw the bolt.

She watched him in silence as he carefully warmed the teapot and filled it, and placed it on the small wooden tray with the burnt-in picture of the Pied Piper. The tray was a souvenir of a visit to Hamelin. For some reason her mother had always treasured it.

He stood politely aside to let her precede him into the drawing-room. When she had poured out two cups, he leant back and smiled.

'Now to business,' he said briskly.

'Five minutes, you said,' retorted Rachel Steiner.

'Or maybe ten. It is a strange story.'

'I'll bet it is.'

He leaned forward earnestly.

'Believe me when I say that I know how worried you are about your parents. Who wouldn't be? A terrible predicament indeed. Quite terrible.'

He paused momentarily, and shook his head, watching her with his alert, unblinking brown eyes. She thought, biting her lip, that his eyes and his gait were the only alert things about him. Otherwise he looked nondescript, characterless. Soft brown hair, softly contoured face, podgy nose and chin, and the sickly, muddy complexion she had noticed when she had met him before.

He must have noted some movements of her lips, for he went on quickly, almost triumphantly:

'But I bring you good news!'

'That would be a change,' said Rachel Steiner bitterly.

'Listen carefully to my great news! I know a sea captain in a certain port – ' he raised his hand warningly – 'don't ask me his name, or where, because I am under an oath of secrecy not to reveal it, who for a certain sum of money is prepared to take your poor father and mother aboard his ship. He is bound for a South American port – don't ask me which – and sails in three days' time. Is that not wonderful!'

Oh, God, she thought, I can't go through with it. I can't carry on with this farce. He doesn't know they are dead, and I didn't know he was alive. Is this reality, or is it a nightmare? If only there were some sound from outside, if only daylight would come. Two hours to daybreak. Perhaps less. The trembling returned to her body. She tried to repress it, clenching her fists, and holding her breath, but her efforts were useless. At once he was all concern.

'You are still cold! Look, I will switch on the electric fire.'

He leant forward and did so, and lifted it, and brought it closer, so that its warmth reached to her stockingless legs.

She parried the reference to money and, summoning all her will-power, tried to appear like a person to whom a sudden and brilliant idea had occurred. Anything to play for time, to tag along with him, not to make a direct enemy of him. He had revealed himself to her to the extent that he was willing for her to know that he was still alive.

To that extent he was in her power, and knew it. He has killed once, she thought, and if he considers it essential he will kill again. So now she said loudly, excitedly:

'But if you are alive, Mr Draper, there is no case against my father! Don't you see!'

He flicked his tongue along his lips and frowned.

'No case against your father, isn't there? There might be, you know.'

'But if you're alive – ?'

'Somebody was still killed, you know.'

She had an impression that the real Draper was beginning to peer out from behind the screen. His voice was not quite so smooth, his speech was quicker, more slick, the words pattering out without hesitation. Even his manner had changed slightly. He was sitting on the edge of his chair, quite still, his watchful eyes never leaving her face. Like herself, he seemed to know that a climax was approaching.

'Somebody was still killed,' said Draper again. 'You can't get away from that, can you?'

'Who was killed?'

'Don't know. Some poor bloke. Some poor bloke who had as much right to live as you and me, hadn't he? See what I mean? A bloke was killed, and Mr Steiner's done a bunk.'

'Why should he have wanted to kill this man?' asked Rachel Steiner in an indignant tone.

Draper side-stepped the question.

'I never said Mr Steiner killed him, did I? I wouldn't be

trying to help him, if I thought he was a murderer, would I? I wouldn't be trying to arrange this passage to South America if I thought he was a murderer, would I? Murder's a serious crime,' said Draper solemnly.

The hypocrisy was too much for her. The moment she had spoken, she wished she hadn't but the words flared out almost without her knowing it:

'So is blackmail!' she snapped, and adjusted her up-tilted spectacles, and stared at him.

He said nothing for a moment. He sat so still that he seemed to have stopped breathing. Suddenly he reverted to his former soothing manner.

'Doctor Steiner, those are harsh words, aren't they? A little cruel?'

He nodded his head slowly, watching her, his gaze moving over her face.

'So you know about that, do you?' he said. 'It has always seemed to me strange that what you call blackmail is regarded with such horror.'

He relaxed a little, and a smile appeared on his soft, shapeless face.

'There is so much cant talked, isn't there? Don't you think? All the time, people are using – shall we call it inside knowledge? – yes, inside knowledge to relieve other people of money, quite often to ruin them in large numbers. I need only mention the Stock Markets as one example. And does anybody object? Is there talk of crime and prison?'

He sighed, and shook his head.

'Sometimes I don't understand human nature, really I don't.'

'I am only pointing out that whereas my father had a good motive in the eyes of the police to kill you, in the case of the –'

'He may have had a good motive to kill the other man, may he not? It's not impossible, is it? He may –'

'Can't you listen!' she suddenly shouted at him. 'Can't you damn well listen a minute!'

He looked at her in a hurt way, and moistened his lips.

'Of course, I can listen. I am listening.'

She realized that she had to keep a tighter control over herself. She forced herself to think more calmly, more clearly. She said to herself: he is a murderer, but the police don't know it. To the police he is dead, just as Daddy and Mummy are dead. They only connect him with the crime as a victim. He could kill me here and now, and they would have no more reason to connect him with my death than with the death of the first victim. He thinks he has a hold over me. If he knew the truth, that he had revealed himself for nothing – what then? She had to go on talking, make some arrangement. If she could get round to the money, then she could win.

She passed her hand over her forehead. She had to go on arguing as though her parents were still alive. She had to make herself think and believe it, in order to sound convincing. So the shoes were still of use, the woollen dress only temporarily laid aside, the photograph a valued treasure, the fountain pen back again on the mantelpiece. She heard herself say:

'If, as you say, you are trying to help my father, perhaps you will tell me why?'

'Because it suits me, see?'

The tone was pert, a little defiant. He was back to his sharp, alert manner. She said:

'Don't you see that if you came forward and told the police that you had only been away on holiday, that you hadn't seen the newspapers, it would at least help. You could do that, couldn't you?'

'I could, but I won't,' said Draper blankly. 'And I won't because it suits me to be dead. See? I'm being frank with you. You can't say I'm not being frank with you.'

He was right out in the open now. The screen had dropped completely. What's more, he knew it. She saw the muscles tighten at the corners of his small mouth.

'I'm going to South America, too,' he added, and she thought: so that's it, there probably is a ship, and he probably does need the money for that purpose.

'And if my father gets arrested, what then?'

'It'll be just too bad, that's all.'

'You mean you would let him be tried for murder – for killing you?'

'That's right,' he said approvingly. 'You've got it dead right. It's Number One first in this world. I wouldn't particularly wish it to happen, mind you, but if the breaks went that way, it would be too bad, wouldn't it? Nobody looks after you but yourself in this world, that's one thing I've learnt.'

Suddenly she realized that in a way it was she who had the upper hand. He needed money. And he thought she had it. She said viciously:

'I'd never met anybody really evil, till I met you.'

'You don't want to get too damn rude,' he snapped, in a suddenly harsh voice. 'I should mind your step, if I were you.' His face suddenly flushed red. 'I could be across at you in one bound, and throttle the life out of you, you bitch.'

He jumped to his feet and stood over her, and for one panic-stricken moment she thought she had gone too far. Then she heard him say:

'I could ransack this house, and then I could tip off the police about where your father is hiding, couldn't I, eh? I could do that, couldn't I? I could do all sorts of things, because I'm dead, see?

'You don't seem to see the beauty of it. I'm *dead*, I don't *exist*, and anybody who says they saw me was just seeing a ghost, got it?'

'Sit down,' she replied, trying to make her voice sound calm. 'How much money do you need?'

He relaxed at once, and seated himself.

'That's better,' he murmured. 'That's more like it. That's being reasonable. People have got to be reasonable. I'm a reasonable man myself. Six hundred pounds.'

'That's absurd. I haven't got that much in the world.'

'I have a message from your – ' he began, but she was never destined to learn what that so-called message was, because at that moment the telephone began to ring, shrilling loudly and insistently through the house, as jarring as it was unexpected.

The instrument was on a small table by Draper's side. He looked at it, then at Rachel Steiner. For a few seconds, they were united in a mutual shock. It was as though the telephone were a living thing which had been hiding while they talked and had now sprung out on them.

So strong was the impression that the instrument was alive that Rachel Steiner unconsciously lowered her voice when she said:

'It may be a transatlantic call. It may be my brother. He was due to arrive today. He may have been further delayed.'

He nodded, and she got up and made to walk round his chair to get at the instrument. But he lifted the receiver for her, and held it out to her, the flex stretched across the front of his body. Thus she had to bend down slightly to be able to put the receiver to her ear.

Robert Draper heard quite distinctly what it was all about.

It was a national newspaper. Very apologetic. Lateness of hour, etc. Rules against intrusion on private grief, but circumstances somewhat unusual. Out of the corner of her eye, Rachel Steiner saw Draper lean forward to hear better.

Had she any statement to make? What sort of statement? Oh, anything. Did she intend to fight to clear her father's name? Devote her life to it, spend her last penny to that end? Something like that. She did not consider it necessary? Did she agree that anybody who had known her father would realize that he could not have been guilty? She did? Then she did, in fact, confirm the rumour that he was dead? Thank you very much.

He took the receiver from her and replaced it, and got to his feet.

'That was rather a pity, wasn't it?' he said regretfully, his eyes flickering over her face.

He knew now that he had no hold over her. He also saw that she knew it. He saw her shrink from him.

She thought: Oh, God, he's going to kill me. Oh, God, I'm going to die. Daddy. Mummy. Julius. Why had Julius been delayed? Why wasn't Julius there? And only an hour before daylight.

Chief Detective Inspector Morgan subsequently fixed the time of the telephone call as approximately 2.50 am.

*

In his official report, the Inspector wrote:

'Although it appeared just possible that financial stringency might induce Robert Draper to risk an approach to Dr Steiner, as he was ignorant of the death of her parents, and therefore believed that he might have some hold over her, the contingency seemed sufficiently remote to preclude the detailing of plain-clothes officers to keep this woman under constant observation.

'In the present shortage of Metropolitan Police officers, and in view of other and more urgent work, it was decided that in the circumstances it would be adequate to request the Hampstead uniformed police to pay some attention to the house after the hours of darkness.

'At approximately 2.25 am on the morning of June 9th, P.C. Taylor observed a light in the drawing-room of the house in Risburgh Road. In view of the lateness of the hour, he investigated, and was able to observe through a chink in the curtains the woman Steiner engaged in conversation with an individual who answered to the description of Robert George Wood, alias Draper.

'Realizing that these houses have a back door which leads on to a lane, he considered it advisable to proceed to a telephone kiosk twenty yards down the road, and telephone the station. He was subsequently joined by Sergeant Strong, and Police Constables Stapleton and Morrow. The latter two officers having been placed to cover the back door, Sergeant Strong and P.C. Taylor knocked and requested entry to the house.

'As had been anticipated might happen, Robert Draper made an attempt to leave the premises by the back door, but was apprehended and agreed to accompany the officers to the police-station. P.C. Taylor stayed with the woman Steiner until the arrival of Woman Police Officer Edwards, since the former woman appeared to be in an hysterical and shocked condition, and had what appeared to be bruises on her throat.

'At approximately 8 am on the morning of June 9th, I saw Draper at Hampstead Police Station, and said to him: "I have reason to believe that you can assist me in certain inquiries I am making into the death of Joseph Parsons, at 127, Paton

Street, Notting Hill Gate, on the night of June 5th–6th. What have you to say?"

'He replied: "I don't know anything about that job. I was with Gladys Turner from about seven o'clock until long past midnight. Her husband often works at night. I have been going with her. She will bear me out."

'I informed him of the death of Mrs Turner, and he replied: "I don't believe it", repeating these words twice in succession. He appeared to be in a distressed condition.

'At approximately 2 pm on the same day, I charged him with the murder of Joseph Parsons, and he replied: "There's been some mistake." '

The trial of Robert George Wood, also known as Draper, took place at the Central Criminal Court on October 10th. According to reports which appeared in the newspapers, one of the key witnesses was Thomas Perkins, described as a former employee of Joseph Parsons, and now of no fixed employment or abode, who gave evidence of Parsons' intention to visit Draper on the night in question.

Draper's defence was that he found Parsons dead in the flat, and decided to create the impression that the body was his own. Being hard pressed for money, he had contemplated setting fire to the flat in order to claim insurance money in respect of his personal possessions, and to this end already had some petrol and candles on the premises.

He agreed, under pressure, that he had thought that a Mr Otto Steiner, occupant of a shop beneath the flat, might well be arrested for the crime.

Under further cross-examination, he could not explain how the man Parsons had gained admittance, but supposed that the door had been accidentally left ajar by a charwoman who periodically visited the flat to clean it.

The jury, after a retirement of thirty-five minutes, found Draper guilty, and he was sentenced to death. His appeal, on the grounds of misdirection of the jury, was dismissed, and two days before the date fixed for his execution, the Home Secretary announced that having carefully considered the case, he could find no reason to interfere with the course of justice.

Contrary to what so often happens, Robert Draper lost considerable weight in prison, appeared to be in a depressed and at times distraught condition, and continually demanded to see his legal advisers and the prison chaplain.

It was not until two months after his execution that an attempt was made to pawn a square gold wrist-watch of Italian manufacture at a pawnshop in Whitechapel Road. Recognizing the watch as one still appearing on his police list, the astute and observant pawnbroker made some excuse about ascertaining its value more closely and telephoned the police.

Later, a man calling himself Harry Perkins was questioned, and, his room being searched, a number of other objects, such as a silver fountain pen and a gold cigarette lighter, all the property of Joseph Parsons, were found upon the premises.

Interrogated by Chief Detective Inspector Morgan, Perkins stated that he had found the objects in Parsons' desk, that Parsons owed him a bonus for some special service he had once rendered him, and that he had therefore purloined the articles.

He agreed that it was odd that a man should put these personal belongings in a desk, and go out of the office without them.

He denied having accompanied Joseph Parsons to Paton Street, denied that he had a grievance against Parsons or that he quarrelled with him while waiting for Draper. He denied sending anonymous postcards or that he had tried to be subtle by indirectly suggesting that Parsons had killed Draper and then disappeared, and he denied that he had slipped up by describing Parsons too accurately.

Finally, he challenged the police to produce any evidence against him, and to detain him further. As he walked out of the police-station, he was so sure of himself that he turned and winked at Chief Detective Inspector Morgan.

'Going to open the whole of this 'ere Paton Street case again?' he asked. 'What a 'ope!'

*

There was only one point which puzzled Shaw. He could not see why Draper gave Mrs Turner as an alibi when she was already dead.

'It was in all the papers, sir,' he pointed out to Morgan.

Morgan thought of Len doing twenty years which meant he would be out after fifteen, perhaps earlier. Still it was enough. Insects who won't get out of the way must expect to get hurt.

'Oh, that,' said Morgan wearily. 'I reckon Draper was only interested in reading about himself. There wasn't much published about Len Turner. Only a small paragraph. There was nothing of interest in Len's case.'

Good old Len was never cut out to make big headlines. He wasn't important in the Paton Street Case. Small stuff. Churned up by the police machine and tossed aside.

He wasn't of even minor interest to anybody by the end of the year – not even to himself.

Other Penguin crime books are described
on the following pages

FAMOUS TRIALS 9: ROGER CASEMENT

H. Montgomery Hyde

The trial of Sir Roger Casement, for attempting to seduce Irish prisoners of war in Germany from their allegiance to the Crown during the First World War, contains features which can scarcely be paralleled since the reprehensible trial and execution of Sir Walter Raleigh.

Casement was twice honoured for his work in the British consular service, and his reports on Belgian exploitation in the Congo had created a sensation. A few years later, with Britain at war on the Continent, Casement was convicted of high treason and hanged. The use – to discredit the defendant – of the notorious Black Diaries, with their allusions to Casement's homosexual activities, has been a source of bitter controversy ever since.

In this revised edition of his original account Mr Montgomery Hyde offers the reader a definitive record of a State trial of outstanding political importance. Much new documentary material, including Casement's diaries, became available in 1959, and this volume contains a representative selection of entries from the hitherto unpublished diary of 1911, as well as Casement's interrogation at Scotland Yard.

Another Penguin by John Bingham

MURDER PLAN SIX

Murder Plan Six, described by the *Evening Standard* as 'a thriller of a very high (and rare) order', is by John Bingham, whom many will remember as the amiable father of Charlotte Bingham in *Coronet Among the Weeds*. If the story is rather less than amiable, it is nevertheless rather more than unusual, with its introduction of Victor Gollancz, the very real and very well-known publisher, as one of the main characters, together with two fictitious authors of the Gollancz 'stable' and two women, of whom one is an angel and the other the very devil. When a note of madness creeps in – happily among the fictitious characters – things are bound to get out of hand, and they do it with a tension that winds up tighter and tighter as time and the tape-recordings run out.

'A much better hand at the novel of murder than Agatha Christie' – *News Chronicle*

'Bingham is as original as Miss Christie is orthodox. The maximum tension and conviction' – *Daily Telegraph*

NOT FOR SALE IN THE U.S.A.

For a complete list of books available please write to Penguin Books whose address can be found on the back of the title page